BEAST OF BLOOD AND ASH

DRAKARN MATES
BOOK 6

KATE RUDOLPH

OMVAR

I prowled the city's paths, wings tucked tight, senses razor sharp. Suspicion clung to me. Every glance was a dagger, expecting violence, despising my presence. This place was nothing like Ignarath, but there were echoes of the distrust. They call me friend, but I hear the hiss behind it. Outlander. Unworthy. I'd never be one of them.

But I'm not here for their trust.

I'd lied when I told Zarvash why I was helping him.

I'm on the hunt.

The river carved through the city, cold and relentless. Its chill soaked into the black stone despite the natural heat of the caves. Scalvaris hunched over that current: bridges, ramparts, walls pressed tight to squeeze out anything that didn't belong. Anything like me.

Younglings cackled where the water fanned out, their scales soft, wings flapping. They were unscarred, foolish enough to think play kept the monsters away. I watched from the shadows. My tail twitched.

One child stilled, bright green eyes locking on me. He ducked behind a bigger girl, red-scaled, sharp chinned. Smart. Survival meant knowing where and when to hide.

A cold draft stirred the river, its glow shifting like fireflies. Brief, savage beauty. I could almost be seduced into staying there all day.

Her scent found me first, sweet, alien, cut with copper and fear. Human. Not just any.

Reika.

I'd trailed echoes of her through twisting alleys, always a step behind. More than once, I thought I'd found her, only to wind up empty. But that scent anchored me. Warm skin, sweet, impossible softness.

My fangs itched. Hunger, hot and unwelcome.

Then I saw her. Across the bank, haloed in the river's glow. Small, vulnerable, but her stance was tight. Hair shorn short, arms moving with careful deliberation. A human at ease is a lie.

She never stopped watching for trouble.

I drank her in. A mistake. Every line, her shadow, the tension under her skin, set my scales twitching. I remembered her scent on desert wind, remembered sand baking it into my bones. I'd chased that trail, let hope and fury tangle me.

Now, seeing her alive, the old need flared.

She crouched at the water's edge, hands busy with a woven satchel, sunlight catching on her arm. She moved like someone who expected the world to collapse. Every motion carved by hardship. I tasted guilt and hunger, burning together.

And then another voice cut through.

"Reika, let's go."

Another human: taller, golden skinned, jagged with vigilance. I didn't know her name. Eyes sweeping, never lingering.

Reika's head snapped up and she saw me. Her eyes widened a fraction before she turned towards the other human and nodded, saying something I couldn't hear.

The taller woman murmured, "Come on, we have to go."

They moved past the Drakarn children, who

splashed aside. Reika glanced back, only for a second, and not at me, then let herself be drawn to where more humans huddled under a carved arch. The city closed around them.

I stayed, claws curling until pain replaced need. I'd crossed half a continent, risked everything, trailing her scent like a curse. I got only her back, her silence.

But the hunt wasn't over.

She was alive. That knowledge settled, a dark comfort, hissing under my skin, fueling the ache that never quite settled.

She was alive.

And for now, that had to be enough.

1

REIKA

MY LUNGS IGNITED, each bitter mouthful of air a rasp of volcanic glass down my throat. Blood. Cold. The acrid reek of my own fear. That's all I tasted. The world above the mountain's ridgeline: pure shadow and silhouette, jagged black slopes tearing at a bruised, starless sky. The wind was a fistful of needles through my clothes, carving into the raw flesh of my arms and my shins.

I had to run. Because when I stopped, when the pain bloomed hot and ugly, a pulsing knot beneath my skin, the guttural voices behind me swelled.

Closer and closer and closer.

Wings beat high above me. Claws scraped stone. Alien. Wrong. The sound vibrated somewhere deep below my ribs, a place only nightmares and old, cold panic could touch. They weren't trying to be quiet.

The monsters who ruled this world didn't have to be quiet when they hunted.

A shard of rock bit my ankle. My blood seeped through the torn fabric of my pant leg. I had to ignore it. I pumped my arms, my body a traitor, screaming weakness back at me even as I willed it forward.

I tripped. I caught myself. Hands scraped raw, stinging, the smell of copper, metallic and sharp as a freshly whetted blade, filled my nostrils.

Keep going. Don't look back. Don't fall.

But falling was all I'd done since the crash. Down. Down. Down. From sky to rock. To cages. To the suffocating darkness behind my own eyes.

A gash across my knee shrieked with each stride. Behind me, the rhythm of pursuit stuttered and one broke off, circling.

Herding.

Sideways, into even rougher terrain. I couldn't fight them *and* the mountain.

A flicker ahead, a wedge of deeper black. A narrow cut in the rock. Shelter? Or a trap? I veered anyway. Feet skidded, palms dragged across rough, unforgiving stone. Wind snatched my breath. This place was hell.

I wish I had died in the crash. At least then it would be over.

The voices grew. That guttural Ignarath lilt, sharp edged with laughter that wasn't human. Too deep. Too sure. One word found me, slithered like a snake through memory. *Little prey.* A name their kind used when they wanted me to flinch.

No. Not again. Not. Ever.

My heart hammered against my ribs. I dove, scraping sideways into the crevice, knees first, shoulder striking stone hard. Stars exploded across my vision. The world shrank to a pinprick. A prayer. A desperate, burning hope. If I could just make myself small enough. Quiet enough—

An arm that was all scale and bone and hardened calluses snaked around my chest. Massive. Immovable. A cage of flesh and strength.

A hand clamped over my mouth. Air ceased. The reek of Drakarn heat, of copper and something old and burnt, suffocated me. I thrashed and got nowhere.

He was a wall. A mountain. A fate carved in scales and ash. My scream died in his palm. My life shrank. Became the thunder of my own pulse, the grit and taste of dirt on my tongue.

I kicked. Bit. Fought the sob tearing at my throat. My vision flooded with scaled red, fierce, impossible in the utter dark. A glimpse of eyes. Burning gold. He leaned in. His breath a furnace blast against my cheek, stinking of ash, of raw hunger and old, cold metal. His fingers flexed. Once. Just enough.

Blackness surged and swallowed me.

I landed back in my body with a jolt so violent the world splintered around me.

A scream tore itself from my throat. Too loud. Far too loud in the stifling dark. My back slammed against stone. Legs tangled in rough, coarse sheets. Sweat, glue sticky and chilling, clung to every inch of my skin.

I couldn't move. Couldn't breathe.

The slab of stone that passed for a bed here felt like a coffin. The blanket, a noose cinching around my knees. Air thickened with sulfur, with the remembered stench of panic.

My heart thrashed, trying to claw its way out through my teeth. Mouth gaping, lungs seizing, refusing to drag in air. I groped for the wall. Stone. Just stone. Not scales. My hand scraped over the uneven surface, knuckles throbbing as if they'd been flayed. No crevice. No mountain wind cutting through me. Not the mountains. Not their hands.

Then there was movement beside me. A soft thump. Bare feet on stone. The crumple of a blanket yanked aside. I twisted, vision blurring, a nauseating swirl of shadow and a soft glare of light. The heat crystal on the far wall burned like a distant, dying fire, its faint glow lining sharp cheekbones; hair shorn close, a human face. Not a Drakarn.

"Reika, hey." Kira's voice. Human. Familiar. Small and gentle around its edges, nothing like the guttural thunder of my nightmares. "It's all right. You're safe. I'm right here." Her words were a tentative balm, and this wasn't the first night she'd had to utter them. "It's all right."

Safe. Such a goddamn lie.

At least I'd only woken her. Kira had her own nightmares to keep her awake.

Whole-body shudders knocked my teeth together, breath coming in ragged, tearing gasps. My terror ricocheted inside me, refusing to be silenced. The world pressed in, stone on one side, Kira's presence a fragile barrier on the other.

I was burning. I was frozen. Veins flooded with icy pain and scorching memory.

I jammed my fist against my mouth, swallowing back more noise. I didn't dare call it a sob. If they heard, if anyone heard …

Oh god, they'd send me back.

Kira's hand found my shoulder, warm against the clammy skin above my collarbone. She didn't squeeze. Just settled, light, present, patient. I flinched, a purely instinctual recoil, then froze.

Guilt, hot and sharp, burned up through the panic. Touch used to mean pain. Always pain. But I wasn't there anymore. Kira was my friend. She wouldn't hurt me.

"It's just me." She shifted closer, her small warmth pressing near. "You're in Scalvaris. Your room. You're with us."

For a moment, her words were just sounds, bouncing off the inside of my skull without sticking. My body screamed otherwise, every nerve ending, every muscle fiber wired for flight, for hiding, for the snap of teeth coming through the dark.

I stared at her hands—broad, callused fingers, nails chewed to the quick. Human hands. They brushed tangled, sweat-damp hair off my brow. Her skin, dry and warm. Not slick with scales. Not carrying the old copper stench of Drakarn blood.

"It was just a nightmare. That's all."

Just a nightmare. As if the line between dreams and memories meant a damn thing anymore. As if old pain didn't keep scoring new, deeper grooves inside me, making it impossible to breathe.

I blinked, forced breath into my chest. Choked on it. The room pressed in, all dark stone and the lingering tang of sulfur, the sick-yellow glow of the heat crystal casting monstrous, dancing shadows.

I tried to see it as refuge, not cage. Failed. Miserably.

My legs jerked in a frantic attempt to twist free of the sheets. Kira's hand dropped away. "Hey." Her voice, a soft anchor. "You're okay. Nothing's going to hurt you here."

I squeezed my eyes shut and willed the demons away. The panic ebbed. Barely. I managed a nod, and Kira backed off.

That was good. I didn't need to bother her with my craziness.

The dream clung to me. Sticky and too bright. I could still smell the phantom scent of blood on stone. Still tasted metal, coppery and foul, on the back of my tongue. My knee throbbed where it had slammed into rock. I brushed a trembling hand along my leg, only to find smooth, unbroken skin. No blood. Only a ghost of an old pain, a deep ache shadowed by memory.

The old terror flared, sharp and biting: What if *this* was the dream and *that* was real? What if I woke up somewhere worse, chains, blades, that deep, knowing laughter in the endless dark? Any of them could walk in. Drakarn, with their slow, predatory gazes, with claws that could pin you like a beetle to the stone, dissecting your fear. If you made noise, drew attention— No. No. No, no, no.

I hugged my knees tight to my chest and pressed my mouth hard into the silky fabric of the blanket, fighting back new tears, new screams that clawed at my throat. The dream skittered at the edges of my vision. Every time I blinked, every time the darkness in the room thickened, it tried to wrap itself around me. I tasted fear, metallic and thick, a bitter poison all the way to my toes.

You're safe. You're here. You're safe.

But safety was always an illusion. A cruel, fragile thing. And I'd learned the hard way, what happened when illusions broke. So I stayed curled in on myself, holding back the storm that raged inside, begging my body and my fractured mind to believe the lie just for one more night.

begging my body and my fractured mind to believe the lie just for one more night.

2

OMVAR

I SLICED through the throng like a shard of broken glass. Direct. Cutting. An unwelcome intruder. The River Market's towering ceiling somehow pressed down, trapping a miasma of sulfur, sharp and metallic. Sweat, acrid and foreign.

A thousand unnamable scents clung beneath it all. Heat crystals flickered overhead, their soft light an oily pulse on scaled bodies, a quicksilver flash off blades arrayed on merchants' tables. Everything gleamed wet. Everything echoed.

And every eye tracked me. Their stares weighed on me.

My wings stayed folded tight. It was a conscious, burning effort of will. To spread them here would be to shove, to assert a dominance I hadn't earned in this hostile city. I wouldn't give them another reason to spew their hate.

They had enough. More than enough.

Traitor. The whisper was a serpent's hiss. *Ignarath dog. Tainted blood.* Always just loud enough to hear, to flay another strip out of my scales.

A hatchling darted past, eyes wide with fear, scrambling up a stone face to avoid the mere brush of my leg. The crowd parted before me, a reluctant, instinctive yielding to my sheer size, but their retreat was barbed with malice. I kept my gaze level, jaw locked tight.

Show nothing.

This path wasn't random. I'd spent days mapping her routines, etching them into my mind. Learning where she went, when she left the dubious safety of the humans' quarters. Always with others, a small, wary pack. Never alone. Until today. Her faint and tantalizing scent pulled me forward, a hook sunk deep in my gut, dragging me toward the herb seller's stall just beyond the river's sluggish edge.

I'd told myself I wouldn't seek her out. That I would grant her the small mercy of peace.

Another lie. My chest burned with the need to pull her close. My mouth ached, fangs oversensitive with the need to mark. The mate-bond was a molten chain that wouldn't let me keep that silent promise.

It burned.

I rounded the corner where the market path narrowed, the air thickening, and there she was. Small. Tense. Her hands, those fragile human hands, worked with careful, almost painful precision over a display of brittle plants. Her back was to me, but I would know her in any hell. The precise set of her shoulders. The hair cut close, dark against her skull. The way her fingers moved—quick, efficient, delicate. She wore layers, even in this suffocating heat. Protection. Always, always protecting herself.

My bones ached with profound cellular recognition. My mouth watered.

Disgust followed, swift and brutal. Not at her. At myself. At the hunger, this raw, undeniable gnawing. At what I'd done, and what I'd failed to do.

I shouldn't be there.

My very presence was a violation. I shouldn't watch her. But she was etched into me, a pattern I couldn't claw free, no matter how I tried.

Not that I was trying very hard.

I stilled, melting against a pillar of cold, dark stone, trying to become shadow. Other Drakarn surged past, some clutching purchases, others dragging heavy carts of metal or freshly butchered meat toward the deeper, darker tunnels. A human female sat cross-legged on a nearby ledge, weaving something from pale fiber, her movements small, contained. She glanced up, registered my presence, and instantly hunched deeper over her task, a small creature making itself smaller.

And there was Reika. Less than twenty paces. The herb seller, a Drakarn female, scales gone soft and gray with age, spoke to her in that slow, exaggerated drawl some used with humans, as if they were stupid, not just foreign. Reika only nodded, her focus absolute on the bundled herbs in her hand. Even from there, I could see the restless dart of her gaze, always checking her surroundings, alert to every shift, every shadow.

She never relaxed. Never let down that razor guard. Her vigilance was a cold twist in my gut.

I should leave. Turn now. Vanish. Stop torturing us both.

Instead, I stepped forward.

My plan, if the chaotic surge of desperation roiling within me could be called a plan, was to walk past. Just past. Let her see me, perhaps offer a single, quiet word. Show I meant no harm. Show I could be near without breaking her. Begin, somehow, to undo the damage my kind had inflicted.

The damage I had done with my silence, my watching from the shadows when I should have acted.

I circled in a slow arc to approach from the front. Better to be seen coming.

She was inspecting a clump of crimson leaves, rubbing them between her fingers. The motion released a scent like bitter smoke. The old Drakarn female gestured impatiently. "Twelve talins," she said coolly.

"It was ten yesterday," Reika said. Her voice, low, steady, careful. Nothing at all like the screams I remembered.

I moved closer, weaving between bodies, forcing my pace to slow. Her eyes flickered up once, caught on someone else, returned to her bargaining.

The herb seller growled. "Today's price is today's price. Make your choice."

One pace. Another. The crowd thickened. A cart rattled past, forcing me aside. When it passed, Reika had paid, tucking bundles into the satchel at her hip. She was turning away.

No. I still hadn't—

I cut across the path, angling to intersect, feet

carrying me too fast. I forced myself to slow. Soften my steps. Roll my shoulders down.

Don't frighten her. Don't be what she fears.

She looked up.

Our eyes met.

And her scent crashed into me. Sweet. Copper. The land after rain. A thread of fear, sharp as a shard of glass, spiked through it. The mate-bond seized, twisted, pulled tight. My fangs throbbed. My claws itched with the need to claim, to protect. I dug them into my palms until pain bloomed, a steadying agony.

I froze, caught in her gaze. Her eyes widened. Color drained from her face. One hand tightened on her satchel strap, knuckles white. The other drifted to her waist where a blade would be.

But she was unarmed.

The space between us vibrated. Hostility. Memory. The insistent drum of the bond. Market scents receded, overwhelmed by her—her sweat, her fear, her warm human skin.

A violent need crashed through me. To reach. To drop to my knees. To beg forgiveness. To gather her against me until her heart steadied, until I could wrap wings and arms around her, guard her from everything.

But I was what she feared most. Or, if not me, exactly, then everything I represented.

Ignarath. The slave pens. The torture.

I never lifted a finger against her, but it didn't make me any less a monster.

I stared, unable to move, to speak. She was pale, dark circles bruising the skin beneath her eyes. Too thin. Taut as a wire. Beautiful in her wounded fierceness.

My mouth opened. Closed. I reached for something—a word, a gesture. Anything to make her see I wouldn't hurt her. That I was ashamed. That I would carve my own heart out before causing more pain.

"Reika." Rough, my throat scraping over her name.

She flinched as if struck. Her gaze darted past me, seeking escape.

"I—" What? What could I say? "I want—" *To protect you. To serve you. To make amends.*

She took a halting step back, bumping a Drakarn male, who snarled. She didn't look at him. Her breathing, shallow, rapid.

Another step. A third. Tensed to flee.

Merchants passed between us, blocking my view. I didn't move. Couldn't. My hand had lifted, unbidden, extended, claws curled. Savage Ignarath. In that moment, I proved every smear. When they cleared, I dropped my arm. But she'd seen.

Her eyes were wild, whites showing, pulse hammering in her throat. Lips parted, no sound. I wanted to curl in on myself. Disappear. I tried to make my stance non-threatening—head lowered, wings tucked. Ridiculous. I was a massive, blood-scaled warrior, scarred and brutal. My presence terrified even blooded warriors.

Her tongue darted out to lick her lips. "You're from there." The words were brave, even if they were barely a whisper.

The crowd around us had noticed. Conversation shifted, quieted, turned curious, ugly. A squat Drakarn female cast a searing glance from me to Reika. "Ignarath filth," she muttered. "Obsessed with prey."

Another voice, low, for my ears alone. "Animal. The council was mad to let you stay."

I kept my eyes on Reika. Nothing else mattered. Only her ragged breathing, the tension. "I won't hurt you," I said.

The words were foreign, stiff. When had I last tried gentleness? Never. I wasn't much for talking at all. My claws and sword were more than enough.

She didn't believe me. How could she? Her memories were full of males like me, proving Drakarn, especially those from Ignarath, could not be trusted.

I stepped back, giving her space. "The herbs," I tried, gesturing at her satchel. "For healing?" Foolish. Trivial.

"Go away." Her voice, louder now, was thick with strain. Not anger. Terror.

I'd lost count of those I'd killed. Watched others bleed for sport. Participated in cruelty by silence, by obedience. Nothing cut deeper than her fear.

"I'm sorry," I said. Inadequate. A breath against wildfire. "I only wanted—"

"Leave me alone." Shadows on her face. Memory in her eyes, darkness, wings, capture, pain. Memory I'd witnessed. "Please."

The "please" broke me. A plea. From her, to me. As if I deserved it.

I stepped back again. "I'm sorry."

For everything.

She clutched her satchel. The crowd's attention thickened. Some human women gathered, wary, watchful. Ready to protect her—from me.

You are the monster in her story.

I retreated another step, face blank, wings tight. Still, she watched as if I might lunge.

If I could have torn the scales from my body, stripped away the parts of me that sent terror skittering over her skin, I would have. Right there.

My nostrils flared, dragging in her scent one last time. The cursed bond hissed, hungry, insistent. It didn't care about her fear. Demanded claiming, completion.

But that was the real obscenity. That I was drawn to her at all. That fate or biology had tied her to me, a weapon, a killer.

Don't force. Don't break her.

I bowed deeply and stepped aside, clearing her path. "Forgive me," I said.

She darted past, giving me a wide berth, not looking back. I tracked her until she disappeared, her scent a ghost in my lungs. I stood rooted, emptied, pierced by shame.

The market resumed its bustle. Water lapped at the river's edge. A child laughed, the sound bouncing like a thrown stone. The crowd dispersed, spectacle ended.

I was peripheral. A shadow. A curiosity, a weapon, maybe a spy. No one met my gaze.

If the mate-bond was a gift, as legends claimed,

then I was a curse. My existence an assault on her peace. An ugly intruder, huge, scarred, desperate.

She won't look at you. She never will.

I didn't care. I wasn't there to be looked at. Reika owed me nothing. I'd torn myself free of Ignarath for one reason—to be certain she stayed safe.

I would stay in Scalvaris, despite their hatred, the weight of being reviled. Endure insults, whispers, suspicion. Fight their battles if needed, spill blood for a city that would never claim me.

Because staying meant I could protect her. Ensure nothing from my world touched her again.

Not even me.

3

REIKA

TERRA HAD SAID "JUST SHOW UP" at least a dozen times since I'd arrived in Scalvaris. As if my mere presence in the training ring was worthy of applause. As if dragging my broken body from one place to another was some grand achievement to be celebrated.

Today, I showed up.

The training cavern opened up before me, an echoing chamber of grunts and impacts. Dark stone stretched in every direction, swallowing light from the heat crystals overhead. I stood at the entrance, fingers tight around my makeshift staff, watching my people, the humans who were making a life for themselves there, move through defensive drills on our designated half of the space.

"Keep moving!" Terra called, her copper hair gleaming as she circled the group. Her voice snapped with authority, her posture perfectly straight despite the years of fighting, crashing, surviving in that hellscape.

I inhaled, tasting the cavern's thick air. My hand flexed around the wooden staff, rough beneath my palm. The weight of eyes on me pricked my spine.

Don't flinch. Don't freeze. Just move.

The memory of yesterday's market burned fresh. His voice, Omvar, rough and strange, saying my name. His massive frame, red scales catching the light. The way he'd reached for me, and that wild, stupid fear that locked my joints, stealing my voice.

I shook the image away. I was there to train, to reclaim strength in the body that had betrayed me again and again. Not to dwell on terrifying encounters with seven-foot Drakarn warriors from Ignarath.

I knew better than that.

"Reika!" Terra spotted me, her face lighting with approval. "Welcome, I'm glad you made it." She closed the distance between us, ignoring the way I instinctively stepped back. "We're running defensive drills. Kira needs a partner."

I nodded, not trusting my voice. Kira was already moving through the exercise, her small frame belying wiry strength. She held her staff like she knew what she was doing … and like she had a plan to do a lot more. She caught my eye and gave a little nod, not quite happy, but acknowledging.

We were all damaged in different ways.

I slipped the satchel from my shoulder and set it carefully against the wall. The small collection of herbs I'd managed to purchase before Omvar appeared weighed heavy inside, wrapped in cloth. I should have left them in my room, but I couldn't shake the feeling someone might take my stuff if I left it behind. I couldn't let it out of my sight. It was my shield against the dark, my pretend purpose when sleep refused to come.

Learn the plants. Learn to heal. Learn to be useful.

As if anything could fix what was broken in me.

I moved into position across from Kira, staff held at the ready. My muscles could manage this, at least. Basic defensive posture. Weight centered. Eyes forward.

"Begin!" Terra called.

We circled each other. Around us, a dozen other human pairs moved the same way, a dance of survival we'd cobbled together from military backgrounds, desperation, and hard lessons.

The cavern's other half pulsed with the true violence of Scalvaris. Drakarn warriors, massive, scaled, deadly, sparred with unbridled intensity. The clash of bodies sent echoes bouncing off the walls. Each snarl carried, amplified by rage and determination.

They fought with fangs bared, wings occasionally flaring for balance, tails lashing. Their training had spectators, other Drakarn lined the edges, watching, assessing, calling encouragement or mockery.

We humans didn't draw crowds. We were barely tolerated.

Kira lunged. I parried, the staffs connecting with a hard thwack. The impact vibrated up my arms. She was fast, but I was getting faster. The months of captivity had stripped me down, but muscle memory was a tricky bitch.

I'd never been a warrior, but once upon a time, I'd been scrappy.

Sweat beaded at my temples. My focus narrowed to the movement—block, step, strike, recover. The rhythm was meditative. My chest loosened.

I could do this. I could be there. I could function.

"Good," Terra said, passing behind me. "Now switch. Kira, defend."

My next strike came harder, fueled by the smoldering anger I kept banked. Kira met it, her eyes widening slightly. The staffs cracked together. The force shuddered through me, not entirely unpleasant.

There was certainty in this. Black and white. Action and reaction.

"Better," Terra said. "But you're still holding back." She paused beside us. "You need more strength training. And cross-species practice."

My rhythm faltered, and I nearly dropped my weapon. "What?"

Kira missed a block. My staff tapped her ribs, too light to hurt.

Terra's gaze swept the Drakarn side of the cavern. "You need to learn to fight them, not other humans. If something goes wrong, it's the seven-foot-tall lizard monsters we need to worry about." She gave me a grimacing smile. "You need practice against bigger opponents. The kind with wings and claws. Darrokar agreed to let willing Drakarn train with the civilians for two hours each week."

Ice water rushed through my veins, and I tightened my grip on my staff to keep my hands from shaking. "You want us to spar with them?"

"I want you to survive," Terra replied simply. "I'm not talking about warrior training. Just defense."

"That's suicide," I said before I could stop myself. The memory of Ignarath, of that desperate run for freedom with wings beating in the air behind me, of being pinned, helpless, flashed white hot in my mind.

Terra's expression softened a fraction, but she didn't give up. "Darrokar and Khorlar will vet every volunteer."

Kira shifted uncomfortably. "How do we know the 'volunteers' won't just use it as a chance to hurt us?"

"They won't," Terra said with absolute certainty. She had that luxury—her mate, Darrokar, was the most powerful Drakarn in Scalvaris. Her faith was protected by seven feet of scaled muscle and political authority. "Anyone who does more than leave bruises will pay."

"I'm not doing it," I said, the words dropping like stones. I kept my voice steady, betraying none of the panic gathering beneath my skin.

Terra looked ready to argue, but something in my face must have stopped her. She nodded once, tightly. "I can't make you do anything. But I need you to think about it. It will be good for you."

I swallowed the knot in my throat.

Terra left to watch Rachel and Eden. Kira and I returned to drills. My movements became mechanical, distracted by the weight of Terra's suggestion. How long before it became an order?

The wooden staff felt suddenly inadequate in my hands. What good was practice if the enemy could snap your spine with a casual twist? What good were our pitiful human efforts against creatures bred for violence?

The Drakarn side of the cavern grew louder. I tried not to look, but my gaze kept sliding that way, drawn by some perverse fascination. Their matches were brutal, elegant in their savagery. Bodies writhing, twisting, locking together in contests of raw power. Wings snapping open for unexpected leverage. Bloody scales glistening under the heat crystals.

A sudden shift rippled through the crowd. The Drakarn drills faltered, attention drawn toward the main entrance. I followed their gazes and felt the floor drop out from under me.

Omvar.

He stood, massive and motionless, in the arch-way, red scales almost black in the cavern's shadows. His wings were folded tight against his broad back, but even at that distance, I could see the tension in them. His posture was rigid, unyielding. His eyes, those burning gold all-seeing eyes, swept the cavern once, pausing fractionally on our human training area.

My pulse jumped. Had he seen me? Was he looking for me?

Don't be stupid. You're not that important.

The murmurs started immediately. Even the humans stopped to stare at the enormous Ignarath warrior. The name alone was enough to trigger a fresh wave of nausea. They were the worst. The cruelest. The most vicious. And this one … this one had sought me out yesterday.

But those stuttering words of his, that apology … that hadn't been for just anyone. I squeezed my eyes shut. I didn't want to think about Ignarath. About why he wanted to apologize. If I could zap those memories and make them disappear, I'd do it in a heartbeat.

"Traitor," someone hissed from the Drakarn side.

If Omvar heard, and how could he not, he didn't react. He moved into the cavern with controlled power. I found myself watching the way he moved, balanced despite his size, dangerous in his restraint.

A young Drakarn male detached from the group, stepping into Omvar's path. His scales were an iridescent green, his frame lean and wiry compared to Omvar's bulk.

"Traitorous dog," the green-scaled Drakarn called, loud enough for everyone to hear. "Come to spy on our training methods?"

I bit back a gasp. The entire cavern went silent. Beside me, Terra stilled.

Omvar stopped. His expression remained impassive, but something in his posture shifted, a subtle coiling of potential energy.

He said nothing.

The green Drakarn, Kith—I was pretty sure that was his name from the marketplace—circled closer. "The Blade Council may have granted you sanctuary, but we all know what you are." His tail lashed, punctuating his words. "Murderer. Slave breaker."

My skin crawled. The words conjured images I'd spent months trying to bury: monsters with their cruel hands, their laughing eyes as they broke prisoners.

Had Omvar been one of them? Had he watched? Participated?

No.

I didn't know him, not at all. But I was sure of the denial down to my bones.

Omvar's gaze flicked past Kith, unconcerned, almost dismissive. The younger Drakarn bristled.

"Let's see what you can do when you're not in your cheater's ring," Kith demanded suddenly. A challenge. Public. Impossible to ignore.

A ripple moved through the watching Drakarn. This was dangerous ground, a battle for status, for acceptance. Omvar might be tolerated, but he was still Ignarath. Still the enemy.

Omvar's attention returned to Kith. He seemed to consider, then gave a short nod. "If you wish." His voice was low, resonant, oddly controlled. An entire conversation conveyed in three simple words.

He said nothing about the accusation. He'd been a champion in the tournaments of Ignarath, a legend there.

And now he was being called a cheat.

Kith grinned, a feral display of teeth. "Center ring. No weapons. First blood or surrender."

"Surrender," Omvar replied. "First blood relies on luck."

The crowd shifted, forming a loose circle around the central sparring area. Even the humans moved closer to watch, drawn by the spectacle.

I wanted to resist, to flee, but morbid curiosity rooted me in place. I wanted to know what Omvar was. What I was dealing with. I'd been locked below in the slave cages when he competed. I'd only heard about him in whispers. This was my chance to see.

The monster you know is safer than the shadow in the dark.

The two Drakarn stripped to their waists. Kith was a finely built Drakarn, even I could see that. But next to Omvar, he looked like a fledgling. I couldn't stop looking at Omvar's scars. They mapped his torso, his arms, his back under his wings. Old wounds. Battle trophies. Torture.

I knew scars like those. My own skin carried similar maps.

The two circled each other, Kith quick and taunting, Omvar steady and watchful. The crowd's murmurs swelled, and I heard the clink of coins changing hands.

"Begin!" someone called.

Kith struck first, a blur of green, claws extended. Omvar sidestepped, effortless, almost casual. Kith attacked again, faster this time. Omvar blocked, deflected, moved like water around stone. No wasted motion. No posturing.

The pattern continued, Kith throwing himself forward met with precise, minimal defense. It was like watching an animal play with its food. My heart hammered as I recognized Omvar's strategy. He was letting Kith tire himself out. Letting him make mistakes. It was the tactic of a seasoned warrior, not a trainee.

The crowd grew restless. "Fight him!" someone shouted.

Something changed in Omvar's posture. A subtle shift, a gathering of energy. When Kith lunged again, Omvar was suddenly elsewhere, behind him, beside him, moving with impossible speed for his size. His hand shot out, gripping Kith's extended arm. In one fluid motion, he twisted, using Kith's momentum to send him crashing into the stone floor.

The impact echoed. Kith recovered quickly, snarling, wings flaring in challenge. They clashed again, bodies locked together. This time, Omvar didn't retreat. He met strength with strength, and even from where I stood, the outcome was never in question.

Omvar was magnificent.

Terrifying, yes, but there was a brutal beauty in his controlled violence. He fought with precision, restraint—holding back enough to make the match last, but never enough to risk defeat. His muscles bunched and flexed beneath his scales, his movements deliberate, devastating.

I couldn't look away. Couldn't breathe. My heart pounded, blood rushing in my ears. This had to be fear. It would be insane for it to be anything besides fear.

But fear had never made my blood thrill.

So of course my brain had to go and ruin it.

A memory bubbled up, unwanted: a dark cell, pain radiating through my body, the distant sound of fighting. A shadow filling the doorway. One of the guards, Draskeer. Dark scales. Darker eyes.

The cavern's noise surged back, too loud, too close. Bodies pressed around me, human and Drakarn alike. The air thickened, suffocating. My pulse raced, sweat slicked my palms. Too many people. Too much sensation.

"—did you see how he—"

"—Ignarath scum, should never have—"

"—could snap a youngling in half without—"

The words blurred, twisted. The cavern tilted. Stone walls closed in, became an old cell. The crowd's voices rose, merging with the roar of arena spectators.

Watching. Betting. Cheering for blood.

Not here. Not now.

My breath came in shallow gasps. The memory of chains weighed my limbs. Of being helpless, watched, beaten. Of combat with no fair terms, no mercy, no escape.

Terra's face swam before me, concern etching her features. Her mouth moved, forming my name. I couldn't hear her over the roaring in my ears.

I had to get out.

I shoved blindly through the press of bodies, ignoring calls of my name. The cavern entrance beckoned—escape, air, silence. My feet moved without conscious thought, carrying me through tunnels, past storage alcoves, away from voices and eyes and judgment.

When I finally stopped, I was alone in a narrow side passage. I pressed my back against cold stone and slid to the floor, drawing knees to chest. My lungs burned. My hands shook. Sweat dampened my clothes. Shame burned hot beneath my skin.

Pathetic. Broken. Weak.

I'd run from a shadow, from a memory, from the phantom trace of my own fear. And from him, from Omvar, with his controlled violence and his burning, knowing eyes.

The worst part was the confusion. He should have been pure terror, pure nightmare. He was Ignarath. Enemy. Monster. I should have felt nothing but revulsion watching him fight.

But there had been something else. A flicker of recognition? A whisper of connection?

I pressed the heels of my hands against my eyes until stars burst behind them. This was madness. He'd sought me out yesterday. He'd known my name. And he'd looked at me today.

Maybe.

Or I was imagining things.

I wanted to scream, but I choked on the urge. I was screaming enough these days.

A cheer went up behind me. The match was over. I didn't need to look back to know Omvar had won.

NIGHT ON VOLCARYTH wasn't really night at all, not under tons of rock that made this place home. It was just quieter.

I slid out of the human quarters like a shadow, satchel clamped to my chest. Boots silent on rock. No one noticed me leaving; crawling back in was when I'd have to answer questions. Not that anyone wanted to know where the broken girl disappeared after dark.

No one wanted my answers.

The hallways emptied as I moved deeper into the tunnels, away from the set of rooms we now called home. Away from Kira's worried glances and the memory of my humiliating escape from the training grounds.

Everyone had seen me panic. Everyone had watched my retreat.

Pathetic. Weak. Still so broken.

The river called to me, not with words, but with the whispering rush of water, the promise of somewhere I could breathe without the world's scrutiny. Even humans had grown tired of my sharp corners, my late-night screams. I knew they whispered when I wasn't there, trying to figure out what to do with me.

I followed the route I'd worn into memory: chin up, stride confident, bluffing a right to exist wherever my feet landed. Even the Drakarn hesitated to challenge someone who seemed certain of their destination.

My haven waited: a niche carved high above the river, half-hidden in the city's lowest bowels. Stone shelves jutted outward in rough, uneven steps leading toward the water's glow. The river below bled cold air and banished a bit of the heat of Scalvaris.

Water over stone, a lullaby meant to calm. Instead, it made the memories echo—mountains, another night, bodies in pursuit, wings chasing overhead, my pulse a drumbeat of terror.

"Not now," I whispered. "You're fine."

Sinking onto my ledge, I drew knees to chest, the satchel clutched tight. The river churned below, shot through with bioluminescent algae, tiny constellations tracing the current, reflected in slick black stone. I tried to lose myself in the light, following each eddy, each flicker, hoping that if I stared deeply enough, my mind might still.

It never did. Instead, the night brought too many thoughts.

The market with Omvar. The shame of running. They circled overhead, scavengers waiting for weakness. I hugged myself tighter, throat raw with words I could never say, muscles aching with remembered violence.

The river's whisper almost drowned them out.

I unclasped my satchel, spreading the contents carefully on the ledge beside me. The herbs I'd purchased were meager: a handful of mintine leaves, some crimson pods of something called fire-thistle, a cluster of pale, feathery sprigs that Selene used for pain relief. I'd been studying their properties whenever sleep refused to come, a small attempt to be useful, to learn enough to justify my presence here.

The mintine leaves were supposed to help with nightmares.

I'd been steeping them in hot water each night, choking down the bitter brew before bed. So far, they'd done nothing. The terror still found me, wrapping skeletal fingers around my throat, dragging me back to Ignarath, to the cages, to the games they played with us. To the burn of sand beneath my feet as I ran, the sound of wings—

A scrape of claws on stone cut through the silence. My hand snapped the herbs back into the satchel, body tensing, senses stretching.

Two figures moved onto the ledge at the far end, robed in Temple yellow, faces foxlike, green scales gleaming. Forge Temple acolytes. Zealots who believed humans were stains that couldn't be scrubbed away.

They hadn't spotted me yet. I might still slip past if—

My boot caught a stone. One of the acolytes' heads snapped toward me, pupils narrowing.

"Look, Mervath," his voice slithered. "A little human, all alone."

I straightened, hugging my satchel to my chest, spine to the wall. "I was just leaving."

The second acolyte sniffed, lips curled. "You reek of healing herbs. Are you ill, human?" The word landed like a curse.

"No." Too flat. Too small.

Their eyes burned faintly. Mervath's tail sliced the air, agitation unmistakable.

"This area is restricted," Mervath intoned. "No humans are permitted by the sacred river."

"I didn't know." That was a lie. I knew perfectly well this area was borderline forbidden, especially at this hour. If caught, I'd be reported, punished, denied even my small daily freedom. But this place was special. It felt like mine.

I'd risked it anyway.

"You lie," the other one spat, tongue flicking. "I taste it on you."

My hand tightened on the satchel strap, knuckles white. I kept my expression neutral, my spine straight. Don't show weakness. Don't flinch.

"I'll leave now." I took a step toward the passageway I'd come through, but Mervath shifted, blocking my path.

"Temple law requires penance for trespass on sacred ground." His lips peeled back, revealing too-sharp fangs. "Especially from impure beings."

My heart skipped, then raced. "I'll speak with Priest Jalliun tomorrow. Make my apologies formally."

Mervath laughed, the sound echoing off stone.

"You would approach a High Priest? A human?" He moved closer, looming. "You've been here long enough to know your place. Below us. Grateful for the mercy we show in not casting your kind out."

I said nothing. Words were useless against that kind of hate. There were two of them, both taller than me by at least a foot, with fangs, claws, and the religious authority to make my life hell. I couldn't fight. Couldn't run. The only exit was past them or over the edge into the river—a drop I wasn't sure I'd survive.

"Tell me, human." The other one's purr slid closer. "Are you the one who escaped Ignarath? Did you fight in their arena?"

My lungs constricted. Cold sweat joined the pulse of blood in my ears. The roar of the river sounded like the roaring crows, cheering for blood. My blood. A champion's. Their own. It didn't matter as long as the need was satisfied.

"No." My voice barely trembled.

His face split into a cruel grin. "I have a cousin there. He says slaves who fail to learn their place don't last long. Maybe we could learn a few things."

I shrank inward, armor on the inside crumbling. The alcove constricted, air clotted thick. I was caged again, every way out locked.

"Perhaps we should show you the true purpose of the Temple." Mervath's words were honeyed poison. "Cleanse you in sacred fire. Burn away the taint of your kind."

I knew they were just words. Intimidation. If they truly intended to harm me, they would have done it by now. But reason couldn't reach the part of me suddenly back in a cage, helpless, watching others be dragged away, hearing their screams. Knowing I was next.

"Back off." The words surprised me, almost brave, coming from the ruins of my voice.

Mervath's friend snickered. "Or you'll what? Will you call your protectors?" He took another step, claws flicking open. "Do you think they'll happily come from slaking their disgusting lusts with their human mates?"

My back hit the wall. Nowhere left to retreat. My breath came in short, painful bursts. Black spots danced at the edge of my vision.

Not again. Not here. Please. Not now.

"Look, it's frightened," Mervath said, delighted by my reaction.

His friend's claw hovered above my cheek. "I wonder what it sounds like when it screams—"

A shadow fell over us. Massive. Absolute. The

temperature around us plummeted, then surged with savage heat.

Both acolytes went rigid. The acolyte closest to me snatched his hand back as if burned.

"Move away," a voice rumbled, rough, low, dangerous. I knew it.

Omvar.

The acolytes spun around, cowed, some primal order enforcing itself. Omvar filled the ledge behind us, scales smoldering red in the glow, wings half-open, eyes molten gold and fixed on them.

"This is temple business," one of them said, voice cracking. "The human trespassed."

Omvar's reply came soft and lethal. "Did she? Or did you corner someone half your size to feel powerful?"

Mervath's wings flared. "You overstep, Ignarath scum. The Forge Temple—"

"The Forge Temple," Omvar cut in, "would be very interested to know two of its acolytes threatened harm to a guest of the Blade Council." His tail whipped once, the motion so fast it cracked the air. "I'm sure High Priest Jalliun would love to hear how you invoked the sacred fire to terrorize an unarmed civilian."

The Drakarn both flinched.

"We meant no harm," Mervath said, stance shifting to something less aggressive. "We were merely informing the human of proper boundaries."

"She has been informed." Omvar stepped fully onto the ledge. Even hunched slightly, he was enormous. "Leave. Now."

For a moment, I thought Mervath might argue. His body tensed, claws flexing. Then his friend grabbed his arm, yanking him backward.

"Come," he muttered. "This isn't worth the trouble."

They retreated, backing down the ledge toward the doorway they'd emerged from, eyes never leaving Omvar. Mervath shot me a final, venomous look before they slipped away, the sound of their footsteps fading into silence.

The moment they vanished, my legs gave out. I slid down the wall, landing hard on the stone, satchel spilling its contents. I couldn't care. I could barely breathe.

The panic that had lurked at the edges, held back by pure survival instinct, crashed over me in a sickening wave. My lungs were on fire. Tears burned behind my eyes. I curled forward, arms wrapped tight around my middle, trying to hold myself together as everything splintered.

Pathetic. So pathetic. Can't even stand up to two damned priests.

Through the roaring in my ears, I heard the careful approach of footsteps. Heavy, too loud, announcing themselves. Omvar's shadow fell over me, but he stayed back, giving me space.

How long I crouched there, trying to force air past the knot of terror in my throat, I couldn't say. Eventually, the worst of it receded, leaving me hollow and shaking, utterly spent. Humiliated. When I managed to lift my head, Omvar was still there, watching me with those unreadable golden eyes.

"Can you stand?" he asked softly.

Not are you alright when I so clearly wasn't. For some reason, that made me feel better.

I nodded, though I wasn't certain. Pride made me try. My legs trembled but held as I pulled myself upright. The wall steadied me. I must have looked wrecked—tear-streaked, hair wild, body quaking with aftershocks.

My scattered herbs lay between us, crushed and damp. All that precious effort wasted.

"They shouldn't have bothered you." Omvar's

voice was careful, as if speaking to a wounded animal. "Temple acolytes should know better."

I swallowed, throat dry. A click echoed as I tried to speak. "Most of the acolytes follow Karyseth. They hate us. They'll take any excuse to cause trouble." I'd been warned. I'd felt the yellow-robed bastards staring at me in the market. I thought I could ignore it.

Silly me.

"That shouldn't matter. The river belongs to everyone in Scalvaris."

A funny thought from the outsider. "Not to humans." The bitterness in my voice surprised me. "Nothing here does."

Omvar was quiet for a moment, his massive frame somehow less threatening than it had been in the training grounds or the market. He knelt carefully and began gathering my scattered herbs, placing them gently back in the fallen satchel. His huge, clawed hands were capable of crushing stone, yet they handled the brittle leaves gently.

"They're ruined," I said.

"Some, yes." He examined a twisted stem of what I thought was fever-root. "But not all. This one is stronger when bruised."

I stared at him, unable to reconcile this gentleness with everything I knew about Drakarn warriors. About Ignarath champions.

With a final, meticulous sweep of his hand, he collected the last of my herbs and held the satchel out to me. I hesitated, then took it, careful not to let our fingers brush.

"Thank you," I said stiffly.

Omvar merely inclined his head. He made no move to leave, nor to come closer. We stood in awkward silence, the river's current whispering below.

"How did you find me?" I finally asked.

"I didn't." He paused. "I come here sometimes. For the quiet."

We'd both sought solitude in the same hidden corner of this vast city. A strange kinship flickered between us, shocking some of the fear out of me.

"You're shaking," he said.

I was. The adrenaline crash left me chilled and unsteady. I pulled my top tighter around me, bracing for warmth, hating the vulnerability.

"It will pass." Everything does, eventually.

Omvar shifted his weight, wings adjusting behind him. They were beautiful, in their way, the membrane stretched between bone, red as cooling coals. I'd never allowed myself to really look at a

Drakarn's wings before. They'd always been symbols of pursuit, of predatory speed.

"May I …" He hesitated, seeming to search for words. "Would it help if I stayed between you and the passageway? Until you're steady?"

The offer was unexpected. A Drakarn, an Ignarath Drakarn, offering to guard me? It should have been laughable. Terrifying.

It wasn't.

And that was even scarier.

"Why?"

His expression remained unreadable, but something flickered in those gold eyes. Pain? Regret? It was gone too quickly to name.

"Because they were wrong to frighten you," he said simply.

Another wave of tremors overtook me, stronger this time. My body betrayed me once more, a sob catching in my throat. I bit it back, refusing to break completely.

"I can't stop shaking," I blurted out. "I can't … damn it, I'm so cold."

Omvar's gaze never left mine, steady and deep. "I am very warm," he said carefully. "If you wished … I could block the cold from the river."

The meaning was clear: he was offering to hold

me. To wrap those massive arms and wings around me, enclose me in living heat.

If anyone had suggested such a thing yesterday, I would have laughed in their face, then run. But I stood in the aftermath of terror, hollow and raw, desperate for something solid to cling to. His presence was the only steady thing in a world that kept slipping sideways beneath my feet.

I should refuse. I knew I should.

"Yes," I whispered instead.

Omvar moved with the same methodical care he'd shown when picking up my herbs. Two steps forward, slow, giving me every chance to change my mind. He stopped an arm's length away.

I was so cold. And he looked so warm.

Another step, and he was there, right in front of me. Huge. Impossible. His scent reached me, not unpleasant, oddly familiar. Like hot metal and woodsmoke, with something underneath I couldn't name. My mouth watered, and my tongue felt strange, like I'd just eaten a chili but it wasn't spicy —just … tingly.

Slowly, Omvar opened his arms. His wings unfurled, creating a sheltered space between us. I hesitated, heart hammering so hard I thought it might explode. Then, with the last scrap of my courage, I stepped forward. Into his space. Against his chest.

Heat radiated from him like a forge, instantly warming the air around us. I stood stiff, uncertain, hands clasped tightly around my satchel, in between us like a shield. This close, I could see the pattern of his scales, the way they overlapped like living armor. The scars that mapped his body, silvery against the red. Some looked intentional, ritual markings, maybe. Others were clearly the result of battle.

Omvar moved his arms slowly, so slowly, until they nearly encircled me. Not touching. Just … there. I could feel the power in him, even without contact. The strength held carefully in check.

I shivered again, a full-body tremor.

"May I?" he asked.

I nodded, beyond words.

His arms closed around me, and his wings followed, wrapping me in a cocoon of crimson membrane and living heat. I tensed, waiting for the panic, for the horrible sense of being trapped.

It never came.

Instead, something in my chest unraveled, a knot loosening for the first time in … I couldn't remember how long. Omvar was solid, immovable. His embrace didn't trap; it anchored.

He smelled of safety. Of shelter. The hard planes of his chest were a wall between me and a world that wanted me broken.

Without really deciding to, I let go of my grip on the satchel and let myself lean into him. Just a little. My forehead rested against scales that were smoother than they looked, warm as sun-baked stone. I expected them to feel alien, repulsive.

They didn't.

One of Omvar's hands, so large it nearly spanned my entire back, settled carefully between my shoulder blades. The gesture was tentative, as if he expected rejection. Ready to withdraw at the slightest sign of discomfort.

"Better?" he asked, the word rumbling through his chest.

I nodded against him. The shaking had subsided. In its place was something dangerous, the desire to stay there, wrapped in living armor, protected from everything.

"I've got you," Omvar said quietly. "I promise."

In the arms of a monster who should have terrified me, I believed it.

5

OMVAR

I STOMPED through the marketplace and glared at anyone who had the misfortune to stumble into my path. The air in the River Market was always thick, a miasma of sulfur, damp stone, and the thousand unnamable scents of a city carved into the planet's heart. It clung to my scales, a film of foreign sweat and unfamiliar spices I could never scrub clean.

I cared about one person in this Forge-forsaken city, and she wasn't there.

But the imprint of her touch still scalded my scales. I'd stayed up half the night, body primed for more, chest burning, tongue tingling with the ghost of her nearness. The memory of her, small and shivering, fitting against my chest, was a brand.

She was mine, but she trembled in my presence like a frightened animal.

My own form was a torment to her. She'd let me hold her, though. In that one moment of desperate need, she had stepped into my arms. Would she let me again? Could I touch her without the specter of violence rising between us? I couldn't let the thoughts cascade, a torrent that would drown my control.

Control was all I had left.

The market thronged with life under the oily pulse of the heat crystals overhead. Drakarn of every color bargained over lavaforged blades and shimmering bolts of fire-resistant cloth. The sound was a deafening clang and hiss, a symphony of life I would never truly be a part of.

My wings stayed folded tight in a conscious, burning effort. Here, I was a weapon on a leash, an Ignarath dog granted a kennel in the enemy's camp. Every stare I met was a fresh accusation.

I cut a path through the crowd, looking for the only other warrior in this city I trusted not to stab me in the back.

Zarvash was sitting beside his mate, Vega, at a small cluster of tables near the back of the market, tucked into an alcove where merchants sold dried meats and potent, sour-smelling ales. If there was anyone in the city I could count as an ally, it was these two. Zarvash and I had fought side by side in the pit in Ignarath, while Vega posed as his slave and tried to learn as much as she could about the humans held captive in my former home.

He was all dark calm and patient eyes, scales burnished bronze, light flickering off the planes of his face. Vega perched at his side, smaller, paler, her gaze sharp as a blade, red hair twisted up and catching stray beams in a tangled halo. Human in stature, but with a force that made trainees step aside.

I'd suspected she was up to something then. I'd sensed the attraction between the two of them even while they played their parts. But the strength of their bond now was staggering, a current of affection and trust humming in all their glances and gestures. I didn't see how I could have that. Not when Reika wouldn't look at me for more than a heartbeat without fear jumping in her throat.

He sat with one arm draped possessively over the back of her chair, his scarred form a fortress around her. She leaned into his space, a small, fierce human who looked as if she belonged there.

I didn't see how I could have that.

Not when my very presence was a source of terror for the one I was bound to.

Zarvash greeted me with a nod, his amber eyes sharp and assessing. Vega raised one of her expressive human brows, her gaze sweeping over me, missing nothing.

"You're scaring the children." Her voice was lightly mocking. She gestured with her chin toward a pair of younglings who had frozen mid-chase, their eyes wide saucers fixed on my scarred, red scales.

"The children could use a fright." I didn't bother to sit. The rage from the night before was still a live coal in my gut, and I felt too large, too volatile for the small space. I might have looked like an ancient monster, risen from some forgotten lava flow. Good. Let them see it. My tail flicked in restless agitation.

"Your Forge Temple acolytes," I spat the word like a curse, "cornered Reika last night by the river. I don't think they would have stopped with taunts if I hadn't shown up."

The change in them was instantaneous. Vega jerked, her casual posture snapping into coiled tension. Her hand dropped to the hilt of the wicked-looking blade she always wore. Zarvash's eyes narrowed, the lazy possessiveness hardening into a commander's focus.

"Who?" Vega's voice was a low growl.

Zarvash held up a hand, a quiet command for restraint aimed at his mate, not at me. "The river is sacred territory. The Temple—"

"Zarvash!" Vega shot him a glare, the kind that would have cowed a lesser male. He just held her gaze, his calm unflinching, but I felt the ripple of tension between them. Even the best pairs fought with knives drawn when their priorities clashed.

"It is true, *veshari*," Zarvash said, his voice a low rumble meant to soothe her, but his gaze remained locked on me. "The Forge Temple is protective of its domains. She should not have been there without permission."

A guttural snarl tore from my throat before I could stop it. The nearest merchant flinched, pulling his wares closer. "You think it is right to terrorize my …" I stumbled over the declaration.

My mate.

The words clawed at the inside of my mouth, desperate for release, but I choked them back. No one knew what Reika was to me, and I would not reveal it, not there. To name her as mine would paint a target on her back, to claim her in a way she couldn't want.

It would make me no better than the brutes who had enslaved her. I forced the words out, each one scraping my throat raw.

"To terrorize the humans you give sanctuary?"

"Of course not," Zarvash said, his tone clipped. "But the Temple's reach here is long. Karyseth's followers believe the Blade Council's agreement with the humans is an abomination. They see it as a stain on Scalvaris. They will use any perceived transgression as an excuse."

"You should have seen what they did to Orla," Vega muttered.

For some reason, Zarvash gave her a remorseful look.

"They called her impure," I said, the words tight with violence. "They spoke of cleansing her in sacred fire." My claws dug into my palms, the sharp pain a welcome anchor. I imagined those claws sinking into the soft green scales of the acolytes, tearing, rending.

"They sure like that threat." And there was another look at her mate. "But we'll make them pay if they try," Vega promised, her eyes blazing with a fury that mirrored my own. She looked at Zarvash. "Won't we?"

"They will be dealt with," Zarvash agreed, his voice dropping to a dangerous calm. "But not with a public challenge. Not with overt violence that will only fracture the Council further and give Karyseth the ammunition she craves." He leaned forward. "You need to tread carefully. Karyseth holds much sway, and on the matter of humans, she has more in common with your people in Ignarath than she does with us."

"Don't call them my people." I flung the words like knives. My throat locked. Ignarath was blood and scar tissue, home only to ghosts and memories I wanted to burn from my flesh.

Zarvash held my gaze, a flicker of understanding in his eyes. I had heard how he had once hated humans, a fervent follower of the Temple's harshest doctrines. His bond with Vega had carved that hate out of him. He, more than anyone, knew the war I was fighting.

"I will speak to Jalliun," Zarvash said, his tone softening as he looked to his mate. "He's a reasonable priest. He held our mating ceremony." A ghost of a smile touched his lips as he shot a fond look at his mate. "Perhaps he can make the acolytes see reason. He can remind them that an attack on a human under the Council's protection is an attack on Darrokar himself. And on me."

It was a political solution. A slow, careful game of influence and pressure. My entire being roared for a faster, more final answer. For blood. For fear driven so deep into those acolytes they would never dare look at Reika again. But Zarvash was not wrong. An open war with the Forge Temple would endanger all the humans, not just her. I forced my claws to uncurl, my jaw to unlock. I gave a stiff, reluctant nod.

For a moment, there was silence. Then Vega leaned forward. Her gaze was sharp as broken glass.

"Are you watching Reika?" she demanded.

"What?" The question, and the force behind it, caught me off guard. It was still strange to have a human, so small and fragile, speak so forcefully to me. In Ignarath, such a tone would have earned her a beating. Here, it was a challenge.

Her expression didn't soften. It grew harder, fiercely protective. "Don't play stupid with me, Omvar. I saw you in the training caverns when she was there. I saw you at the market the other day. Now you just happen to be there when she's cornered by priests? The assholes you used to call friends nearly killed her. She was hunted in the Harrovan Mountains after she escaped. She still won't talk to anyone about it. She flinches anytime a Drakarn youngling gets too close. So let me ask again. Are you watching her? Because whatever your game is, don't mess with her. Don't you dare break what's left."

Every word was a nail driven into my flesh.

A hot, possessive fury rose in me, the instinct to snarl, to put this small human in her place, to declare Reika was mine to watch, mine to protect.

How dare she question my motives? How dare she imply I would harm her?

Zarvash must have sensed it. His body went still, his hand settling on Vega's shoulder, a silent warning. His eyes fixed on me, no longer allies, but two alpha males on the brink of conflict over territory. The air crackled with unspoken threats. He knew what I was. A champion of Ignarath. A killer. He was reminding me of the predator he saw, and the one he could become if I threatened his mate.

But Vega's words had struck deeper than pride. *She flinches anytime a Drakarn youngling gets too close.* The memory of her body, tense as a wire in my arms, and of the terror in her eyes before she'd collapsed against me, flooded my senses.

Vega was right.

My size, my scales, my past, I was the living embodiment of her nightmares. My presence, meant to be a shield, could be just another cage.

The fire in my gut cooled to a bitter ash of self-loathing. I looked away from them, my gaze falling to the ceaseless, glowing current of the river.

I let out a slow breath, forcing the rage down. "I have no intention of harming Reika."

My voice was flat, devoid of the storm raging inside me. Vega watched me for a long moment, searching my face, before giving a curt, unsatisfied nod. Zarvash relaxed his posture by a fraction.

I turned without another word and stalked away, leaving them in their fragile pocket of warmth and belonging. The market's noise crashed back in, but I heard none of it. I heard only Vega's warning echoing in my skull.

Don't you dare break what's left.

Zarvash could have his politics. Vega could have her warnings. They saw a problem to be managed, a traumatized human to be handled with care. They were wrong. This wasn't a matter of politics or caution. Those acolytes had threatened her. They had put their hands on what was mine.

I would not break her. I would protect her. And

I would not be careful. I would not tread lightly. I would be the shadow that fell over anyone who wished her harm. I would be the monster in their stories, the terror in their night. I would spill blood for a city that would never claim me, and I would raze it to the ground to keep her safe. Let them whisper. Let them hate me. It didn't matter.

The hunt had just begun. And I would not fail her again.

6

REIKA

I WANTED to kill those acolytes.

Fire still blazed through my veins a whole two days later—a righteous, helpless fury that left a taste like scorched metal on my tongue. Two nights of nightmares more extreme than usual didn't exactly help. Not even Kira could calm me down when I woke up, slick with sweat and choking on screams, sure that the sadistic guard Draskeer was about to take a blade to my flesh.

Again.

The memory was a phantom limb, an ache where skin had been torn. I couldn't shake it. Couldn't sleep it off. Couldn't outrun it. So I did the only thing I had left. I went looking for a different kind of pain.

The training grounds were deserted when I entered. The vast, subterranean cavern echoed with the ghost of violence. It smelled of Drakarn sweat and sand that clung to the damp stone and filled my lungs. I squeezed my eyes shut and forced myself not to think of Ignarath.

It didn't work.

The scent memory was too strong. I could almost hear the cheer of the bloodthirsty crowds, a roar that vibrated deep in my bones. Almost feel claws wrapped around my throat, pulling me closer and …

No!

I snapped my eyes open, my heart hammering against my ribs. My gaze darted around the empty space, searching shadows for threats that lived only in my head. This was Scalvaris. The air was warmer there, the light from the overhead heat crystals a sickly, sulfurous yellow, but it was safe.

Or, well, safer.

They didn't have slaves there. The only Ignarath in this territory was Omvar, and he was …

He was …

I didn't know what the hell he was.

Just thinking his name sent a confusing jolt through my system. One part of me recoiled, flooded with the terror of his kind—of the scaly brutes who ruled my nightmares. But another part, a deeper, more treacherous part of me, remembered the solid wall of his chest, the impossible heat of him.

My skin tingled where his arms had wrapped around me, a memory that was both a brand and a balm. The physical reaction was instantaneous and infuriating. A flush crept up my neck, my stomach tightening into a knot that was equal parts dread and a strange, unfamiliar longing.

I hated it. I hated him for making me feel it, and I hated my own body for its utter betrayal.

You are not broken, I told myself, the words a thin, frayed mantra. *You are not broken.*

I squared my shoulders and marched over to the racks of weapons, the grit of the sandy floor crunching under my sandals. They were made for Drakarn warriors and far too big for me. Row upon row of massive swords, brutal-looking axes, and spears that were longer than I was tall. It was Volcaryth's way of reminding us humans didn't belong: fragile, breakable things in a world of stone and predators.

I yanked a staff off the rack and held it up. Heavy, but it would do. The polished wood was rough against my callused palms. I could use the strength training. If I was stronger, maybe the nightmares would stay away. Maybe I wouldn't feel so pathetic.

I moved to the center of the arena, the empty space amplifying the sound of my own ragged breathing. I fell into a basic stance, feet planted, knees bent. I swung the staff in a wide arc, the weight of it pulling at my shoulders, forcing a grunt from my lips.

Again. And again.

I poured all my anger, all my fear, all my shame into the movements. The two acolytes. The memory of their sneering faces. My own humiliating panic. The staff became my fury, slicing through the thick, heavy air.

But my form was sloppy. My frustration mounted with every clumsy pivot, every swing that was just a little off-balance. I was fighting myself as much as any phantom enemy.

And someone was watching me.

The feeling was a cold prickle at the nape of my neck, the sudden, certain knowledge that I was no longer alone. My hypervigilance screamed. I didn't stop my motion, didn't give anything away. I swung the staff in another arc and pivoted towards the entrance, holding my weapon like it was a sword instead of a glorified stick, the end pointed directly at the cavern's opening.

Omvar stood there. Waiting.

He filled the archway, a massive silhouette against the distant glow of the city tunnels. His red scales absorbed the faint light, making him seem carved from shadow and cooling magma. He was perfectly still, his sheer presence a physical weight in the air.

I swallowed hard, my mouth suddenly bone-dry.

I wanted to run. To hide. To dig a hole and crawl into it and never see the light of day again. But I was already living underground, and that hadn't done much to help me face my fears either. I had run from him in the market, run from him after his fight, run from him after he'd held me.

I was so tired of running.

There had to be a bit of boldness in me some-where. A scrap of the person I used to be before all this.

The memory of his arms wrapped around me flashed through my mind. His body shielding me from the acolytes. It was a paradox that threatened to tear me apart.

He was the monster from my nightmares and the only solid thing I'd had to hold onto in months.

"Did you come for the show?" I asked, my voice tight but steady. I held my staff up like a shield, a pathetic piece of wood against a mountain of scaled muscle.

Omvar stepped forward, slow, waiting for my reaction. Another step. Then one more, easy and practiced, until it felt like he took up all the space, his scent spreading—smoke, hot metal, something wild and almost clean. My pulse skittered.

"Would you like a training partner?" His voice was a low rumble, deep enough to vibrate in my gut.

No! screamed some part of me. *Run. He's one of them.*

Yes, a traitorous whisper answered from somewhere deep inside me.

When Terra said I should spar with a Drakarn, I never imagined him. Her words from the other day echoed in my head. *You need practice against bigger opponents. The kind with wings and claws.* She was right. I knew she was right. But the thought of letting any of them that close, of willingly putting myself in that position was … unthinkable.

And yet, I wasn't sure there was anyone else I

could even let try. I'd seen the casual cruelty in other Drakarn eyes. But not in his.

He'd held me like I mattered.

I wasn't shaking. That was a change. My hands were steady on the staff, my feet planted. My heart was a runaway train, but my body held its ground.

"I wouldn't say no to a few pointers." It came out almost sarcastic.

A flicker of something, maybe surprise, crossed his features before being smoothed away. He gave a single, sharp nod and moved to the weapon rack, selecting a staff that looked twice as thick as mine.

He approached me in the center of the ring, his size overwhelming. He demonstrated a simple defensive block, his movements fluid and powerful where mine had been clumsy and forced. "Your center of gravity is too high," he said, his voice quiet. "You fight with your arms. You need to use your whole body. Like this."

He moved behind me. My whole body went taut, every nerve on high alert. I felt the fire of his breath at my ear, the heat pouring off him—not the heat of danger, but something alive.

His hand closed around my upper arm. Claws, ever-present, curved but careful; a threat, but somehow ... familiar. Goosebumps shot across my skin—a reminder of what he was, what I was letting him do. My own traitorous body leaned back, just a bit, into his guidance.

"Keep your weight centered," he murmured, low enough that it was almost private. He adjusted my grip, his other hand sliding to my lower back, pressing me imperceptibly into the stance. Every place he touched me felt raw, hypersensitive. The heat of him against my spine, his chest ghosting along my shoulders, professional, almost, but too much, too close. His thigh brushed mine as he nudged my foot into place.

Instructional, I told myself. Just a lesson.

We returned to position—him opposite me, holding his staff. My thoughts scattered. All I could think of was him, his strength, his restraint, the way he could break me and chose not to.

I fumbled a step and lost my footing. His staff came down, quick, controlled, not hard, but enough to knock my grip loose, my own staff clattering to the ground in the echoing quiet.

I stumbled forward. Into him. And his arms wrapped around me before I could fall.

His arms caught me automatically, closing around my body with heat and impossible gentleness. For a heartbeat, I was wrapped in him: his chest solid beneath my palms, scales radiating warmth, heart beating a steady thrum beneath my hands.

The heat igniting in me was nothing like the blazing anger from before. No. This was need. A raw, aching thing that stunned me with its intensity. I hadn't felt it in months. I'd been certain I'd never feel it again. I'd thought that part of me had been scoured out, burned away by pain and fear.

And for one of the monsters on this planet? For an Ignarath warrior?

Never.

Tell that to my body, which was humming with a life I didn't recognize, leaning into his touch even as my mind screamed in protest.

I tried to focus, to clear my head, but his proximity was a drug. My thoughts splintered. All I could feel was him. The solidness of him. The sheer, restrained power of him. How could I want this? How could any part of me crave the touch of a creature that represented everything I feared?

I didn't pull away. Didn't run.

Instead, I looked up. Up and up, into golden eyes blown wide with something hot and hungry. His gaze dropped to my mouth, the air between us thick and charged and trembling.

The training was over. This was something else, something wild and terrifying and alive.

I was so tired of being afraid. Tired of being prey. I wanted, just for a heartbeat, to choose.

To reach and take.

So I did.

I rose on my toes and curled my fist in the rough fabric at his hip to balance myself.

I kissed him.

Not gentle. Not sweet. I crashed my mouth to his, all rough desperation, pouring in every ounce of confusion, longing, and anger I had left. For a heart-stopping moment, he was perfectly still, a statue of surprise.

Then a low growl rumbled deep in his chest, and his mouth answered mine.

One of his big hands slid from my back to cradle the base of my skull, claws brushing lightly through my hair. His thumb stroked my neck, sending sparks through every nerve ending. The threat and gentleness wrecked me in equal measure.

I pressed closer, desperate for more: his heat, his power, his mouth on mine. Every inch of contact stoked the fire. I was melting, unraveling, alive in a way I'd forgotten was even possible.

He shifted, tilting my head, and his mouth

claimed mine more fiercely, tongue tracing a line that left me shaking—possessive, demanding, but never rough. I moaned against him, swallowing his heat, his need, my own. Thought left me. There was only sensation, surrender and wanting, the bared edge of possibility.

Something brushed my thigh. Smooth, strange, strong. It curled around my leg, up the back, wrapping, holding.

A tail.

A Drakarn tail.

The realization cut cold through the haze, shocking, undeniable.

I was kissing a Drakarn. One of the monsters. Letting him hold me. Letting him claim me as if I belonged.

What the hell was I doing?

I wrenched free, gasping, sucking in air that suddenly tasted like shame and panic. I stumbled back, looking up and up at Omvar, looming in the light, his face half-shadowed, half-fire. His eyes still burned gold, pupils huge with wanting, tail coiled around my leg possessively.

How could I kiss him? How could I want him to touch me?

The panic finally snapped the thread. My body

moved before my mind could stop it. I ripped my leg free, spun, and darted away.

"Reika—"

His voice, ragged with confusion and something deeper, chased me down the stone hall, but I left him behind.

I ran, feet slapping, lungs burning, eyes blurring, away from him, away from myself, away from everything I had just admitted, even for a second, to wanting.

I WAS HER MONSTER.

The thought was a parasite, burrowing behind my eyes, gnawing through the quiet hours after the city's fever heat bled out and left the stone cold against my scales. I did not see Reika again—not after she ripped herself away, not after the brand of that kiss. It was hers, fierce and wild and broken, a last act of defiance before the shame crashed down and she fled. I had stood there, my throat tight with her name, knowing I was the last thing she needed. Wanting anyway.

Now all I had left was the sour taste of her memory on my tongue, the scorch of her scent in my lungs.

I hated myself for wanting. Hated myself more

for being the reason she ran. I was no fool. To taste her once was a blessing I had forfeited a thousand times over. To ask for more would be a gift I did not deserve.

So I did what I had always done when the shame came crawling: went in search of penance.

Scalvaris was forever hungry, demanding bodies to guard its borders against the desert's teeth. The surface patrols were a brutal exchange, warriors trading safety for honor, their wings thrown to the wind as their eyes peeled for enemy blades. No one volunteered without incentive. The twin suns did not forgive. The red waste would strip your scales and bake your flesh before an enemy blade ever touched you. And if that didn't kill you, the boredom would bleed you dry.

I volunteered.

I stood at the flight shaft's edge, talons digging into blasted stone, felt the pulse of life far below. My scales drank the suns' fury, every old scar a ghost of remembered pain.

I welcomed it. I pulled the insignia of Scalvaris tight, a thin strip of battered leather laced with a shard of heat crystal. It was barely earned, barely respected. The stone hummed faintly, a pathetic glimmer against the fire in my gut. Who would see me as anything but Ignarath's mangled hound?

I launched myself anyway. My wings spread open, caught the first hot updraft, and soared above the city that would never claim me.

Base camp was a ruin of sun-bleached boulders and gear half-swallowed by volcanic dust. Water skins hung from a leaning spike, their shadows short and sharp, leaking the very promise of relief. The suns were climbing, turning every rock into a forge. The air itself was a weapon, a wavering distortion that promised to blister tongues and split open scales.

Nyx was already waiting, parked with casual arrogance atop a rock as if he owned the wasteland. His stormy scales caught the sun in fractured, ruthless light. He wore his command like a second skin.

The moment my wings slammed down, kicking up dust, he looked over with a smirk. "Who did you piss off?"

I grunted, rough in my dry throat. "I'm here to help."

He cocked his head, one wing flaring for balance as he stood, his expression unreadable. "Champion of Ignarath, come to babysit recruits?" He let the words hang, a test for bite. "Not what I expected. But I won't complain. Things have been quiet." He jerked his chin at the motley crew by the boulders, a few soft-scaled whelps feigning bravado around a spear rack.

I forced my wings tight to my spine and picked up a discarded shield. "Show me around."

He led me through the camp like I was a visiting dignitary, not a stray let in from the wastes. The tension in my shoulders never eased. Their eyes followed me, the new bloods. Their faces were bright with curiosity and something sharper. Fear. Fascination. The kind of awe you feel for a legend you aren't sure is real.

Nyx leaned in, his voice a low rasp meant only for me. "Don't let their stares fool you. Half of them want your glory. The rest want you gone."

I snorted. "Babysitting children. Maybe that's all I'm good for."

"Keep them alive, and I'll owe you a debt," he said. "That's more than most get in Scalvaris."

I didn't want a debt. I didn't want gratitude. I wanted a purpose that was more than violence, a way to carve out the rot of Ignarath's shadow from my bones.

But I wasn't thinking about Reika. Not now. Not

with the sun burning down like a judgment I could not outrun.

The morning passed in suffocating monotony. Four hours of wind slicing over sand and the slow, steady march of shadows. Long-winged, razor-beaked birds wheeled in the distance, their cries warped by the heat. Each time, a trainee tensed, fingers twitching on a weapon, mistaking simple animals for enemies.

Tarion, the youngest, could not sit still. His scales were a bright, unscarred green, his movements quick with untested energy. He watched me like I was a living myth.

"What's it like in the arena?" he asked, his voice jumping with eagerness.

My eyes stayed on the horizon. The desert stretched into a fractured infinity of red stone and black sand. Nothing gentle. Nothing forgiving. The arena was in my bones, its memory carved into every scar on my arms. I didn't want to talk about Ignarath.

Tarion did not take the hint. "I heard you were champion for years. Undefeated. Is it true?"

I grunted, letting the silence sharpen.

Champion. Pet fighter. Skorai's dog. Survival in that place depended on selling pieces of your soul for one more day above the sand. The price was always too steep.

Tarion looked at me with wide, clean eyes, as if I held secrets he could steal. I remembered being that young, thinking victory meant something more than survival. I didn't have the heart to tell him it did not.

The suns hammered down. Heat seared every breath. My claws dug into my thighs, grounding me in pain. In the now. I had just begun to let my mind slip blessedly blank when the alarm went up.

A sharp, metallic clang echoed over the wasteland, the signal blown through a battered war-horn. The sound ripped through camp. Trainees snapped to attention, faces blanching, weapons drawn with shaky hands. Nyx's eyes flashed.

Interlopers.

We sprang into action. Orders cracked through camp. Wings snapped open. The young bloods fumbled with straps and weapons, some trembling. I launched skyward, heat buffeting my wings, the air already choked with sand.

Pursuit was the only thing that ever felt pure. No past, no fear. Just the hunt. My mind narrowed to instinct: track. Chase. Subdue.

We saw them fast, shadow-shapes streaking over

broken stone, their clothes flapping with the distinctive style of Ignarath. My blood thrummed.

It was a brutal chase, wind tearing at my face, grit stinging my eyes, my muscles burning with ugly memory. The wasteland stretched open. No cover. We drove them forward, our wings beating a frantic rhythm against the oppressive air.

I caught one as he miscalculated a turn. I slammed him down hard, the impact kicking up a plume of black dust. He bucked, cursed in an Ignarath lilt.

My claws pinned him. I looked down, and the face that snarled up at me was no stranger.

Jerras.

Not friend, not enemy. Someone I had bled beside and ignored as he spat on the weak. Everything ugly about Ignarath lived in his eyes: cunning. Cruelty. Certainty. His dust-matted scales were a dirty gold.

"It is true." Jerras scowled, straining under my grip. "Dog. Traitor. Prey-loving scum."

The words should have slid off my scales. They did not. They found every old bruise and dug in deep.

Other trainees circled, their breath coming fast.

Nyx barked a command, but I only had eyes for Jerras.

"Skorai wants his property back," Jerras sneered, his voice pitched for my ears only. "It is time to stop playing."

Property.

He meant her.

He meant Reika.

Ice flooded my gut, an arctic chill knifing through the heat. The mate-bond shrieked, a snarl of fire and panic clawing inside my chest. My world collapsed to the feel of his throat under my hand, the stink of his breath, the absolute threat in his words.

No. Not again.

Jerras twisted, shoving, but desperation made my strength absolute. I heard shouts as other Ignarath fought, the chaos of blades and snapping wings a distant storm. None of it touched me.

This is what I am, the words shook through me. *This is what I am for.*

The world shrank to blood and claws and teeth. My grip tightened. Jerras's eyes flared with panic, but it was too late. I slammed him back into the stone. Claws tore through scales. I felt bone crunch, the hot wash of his blood spilling over my hands. It was a savage, ugly kill meant to send a message.

I didn't care. I needed him dead. I needed them all dead.

I let the rage ride me, snarling through my fangs as the trainees stumbled back, shock and horror on their faces. Let them see the monster. Let them remember there are worse things than exile.

Jerras's last breath rattled out, full of hate. But Skorai would not stop with one patrol.

I let his corpse drop to the sand and looked up, chest heaving. The remaining Ignarath were being herded by Nyx's warriors, stripped of weapons, their wings pinned.

The silence that followed was thick, a bloody echo hanging over the desert. Tarion stared at me, his eyes wide with terror, the myth of the champion shattered.

Good. Maybe it would keep him alive.

My claws dripped red. The bond inside me screamed.

Protect. Find her. Kill everything else.

Nyx stepped up, assessing the carnage with a level gaze. "You finished your business?" His voice was cold, unflinching.

"Not yet." The words came out raw, torn from

my throat. "I need to go." I could not stay, could not explain. There was nothing left but the need to find Reika. To warn her. To stand between her and the storm rolling in from my past.

Nyx nodded once, reading the desperation on my face. "Go. We will take care of the rest."

I took off without another word, wings beating hard, blood trailing in my wake. The city shimmered on the horizon, a promise and a warning. Every muscle in my body screamed with purpose, the only clarity I had felt in months.

Run. Find her. Protect her.

The hunt had begun again. And this time, I would not fail.

Not again.

8

REIKA

I MISSED HOME.

That was a freaking joke.

When I'd boarded that starship, I didn't look back. I'd packed for a new life, not a memory. My bags were filled with practical things, clothes and tools, and not a single photograph or scrap of nostalgia to weigh me down. I'd wanted the stars, any stars, a clean break from the dirt and suffocating cities of Earth.

I just hadn't planned on this place.

Not Volcaryth. Not a planet of monsters, volcanoes, and slavery, nights that pressed in until I couldn't tell the difference between dream, memory, and the shape of my own body clawing free from a too-small room.

The nightmares were getting worse.

I kept waking tangled in rough bedding, sweat turning to ice on my skin. The room stank of fear, the shadow of terror so thick it felt like it should leave bruises. Some nights, the fear seeped into my bones before I even slept, a slow poison creeping in with the drip of water through stone, the distant clang of steel where Drakarn warriors sparred. But lately, it was the dreams that cut the deepest.

And they were making Kira bold.

She sat beside me now, knees tucked to her chest, hair sticking out sideways from another restless night. Kira always watched me like she was waiting for the cracks to show. The heat crystal on the wall flickered, throwing a sickly yellow light across her too-bright eyes. She looked exhausted.

Join the party.

"When you saw Larissa," she started, her voice a fragile thing in the heavy air, "was she doing all right? Vega said she didn't see her, but she's alive. What's it like there? How bad is it?"

Kira's sister, Larissa. Taken prisoner alongside me and every other human unlucky enough to crash near Ignarath. Every day, Kira asked. Every day, I dodged. Today, I was already strung out, my edges raw with panic and the ghosts clinging to the walls.

I didn't want to talk about Ignarath. Didn't want to remember the shriek of cage doors, the screams that echoed through the stone bowels of that hell. I didn't want to taste the sand packed in my mouth or the copper of my own blood, didn't want to see the way the Draskeer and his guards laughed while they bet on how many days we'd last.

But it was there anyway. The memory. Hot and bright. The arena, the snap of whips, the hiss of flesh meeting hot metal. Larissa's face, slack with exhaustion, her eyes dull but stubbornly, impossibly alive. That was all I could ever give Kira. Alive.

I wanted to lie. To conjure some shimmering hope from the dregs of what I'd seen. But I wasn't built for it. The lie would crumble before it left my mouth.

She waited, her silence a twisting knife.

"I don't fucking know! She's a fucking prisoner, what do you expect?" The words exploded out of me, too loud, too harsh. A whip-crack in the stale air that left scorch marks on the silence.

Kira's face flickered. Hurt, then a wall of anger.

She pulled her thin blanket tight, her mouth a bloodless line. "Sorry for asking." Her voice was flat, wounded in that way only someone close can make you feel.

I wanted to take it back. To tell her I was sorry, that she didn't deserve the shrapnel of my nightmares. But the words were there, a lump of jagged glass I couldn't cough up. All I could do was clench my fists, staring at the terror-stained stone beside my sleeping platform.

The silence between us cracked open, jagged and ugly.

Finally, Kira shoved herself to her feet, her movements sharp enough to slice the air. She grabbed her threadbare coat, patched in three places, and fumbled with the door latch, her knuckles turning white.

"I hope you feel better," she muttered, her voice trembling with something I'd put there. "Because I don't know how to help you anymore."

The heavy door scraped open, the scrape of stone echoing the tension in my jaw. She slipped out. She didn't look back.

The slam of the door left me alone. Alone with the choke of sulfur, the pulse hammering a frantic rhythm in my throat. Alone with the small, battered trunk smashed into the corner, as if it could absorb the violence of just existing there.

My hands were shaking. I was going to throw up. Tears burned hot behind my eyes, and I squeezed them shut so tight it hurt. I just wanted to go home.

Why was this my life?

I pressed my palms to the rough stone wall, letting its unforgiving chill seep into my skin, more real than the fire in my lungs. The room was a coffin now, the corners closing in, the walls slick with condensation and the ghosts of a thousand sleepless nights.

You are not broken, I told myself. Again. Again. The words rang hollow, brittle as bone.

Safe is always a lie.

I tried to breathe around the thought, but the stale, sulfur-laced air only burned. It mixed with the scent of wilted mintine and dried fire-thistle spilling from the herb satchel by my bed. I could hear the city somewhere above, beyond the iron-latched door. Water dripping. Muffled voices. Clanging metal. Life going on, uncaring.

My body curled in on itself, knees to chest, arms wrapped tight. I was poison. That was the truth of it. I lashed out, and everything I touched curdled.

The memory of Ignarath rose unbidden, mud sucking at my boots, the throb of blood in my mouth. Drakarn voices, guttural and gleeful, promising pain.

In Scalvaris, they said I was safe. But this stone was just a different kind of prison. Kira was gone. And even there, deep under a city built by monsters, I had nowhere left to run.

The air thickened, pressing in. My heart jerked, a stuttering, frantic bird against my ribs. I squeezed my legs tighter, gasping, sweat slick on my brow. The panic boiled over.

When I opened my eyes, there was a monster in the doorway.

A scream snagged in my throat, a hook in my flesh, unable to break free. I saw blood. A sword. Red scales. Giant wings. The figure filled the entire entry, too wide for the frame, his head ducked under the lintel. His tail flicked with restless, deadly intent.

He was going to take me back.

Oh god. Oh god. No.

I scrambled backward, my legs tangling in the thin bedding. I couldn't move. Couldn't breathe. My body locked down as the monster stepped into my room.

Blood dripped from his blade to the floor, scenting the air with copper and smoke and a wave of Drakarn heat that was too much, burning, suffocating me.

"Reika."

That voice. Deep, a rumble like shifting stone, yet gentle. The sound was a strange comfort, frayed around the edges but careful, as if he knew what fear tasted like.

Omvar.

Though he was covered in blood, he didn't raise his weapon. His massive silhouette pulsed in the heat crystal's wavering light, gold eyes fixed on me, unreadable.

"You need to come with me."

He sounded wrong. Too calm, too controlled for the carnage staining his arms and claws. Muscle flexed under red-black scales as his sword swung low at his side. Blood, some of it his, most of it not, spattered his chest and trickled across the ritual scars that mapped a history of violence.

My mouth worked, but no sound came out. Then I found my voice, a jagged croak. "What?"

He stepped closer, moving with the caution of a man approaching an animal about to bolt. I pressed myself farther away. My herb satchel spilled to the floor, mint and fire-thistle, my only shield, utterly useless.

"It's Ignarath," Omvar said. He sounded like he bit the words in half to keep from snarling them. "It isn't safe."

The world shrank to the beat of my own heart. Ignarath. The name was a blade pressed to my throat.

I drove my back against the icy wall. "No. No. I'm safe here." My voice was a thin thread of sound. My nails dug into the stone at my side, seeking an anchor. I shook my head, again and again. "I'm safe here."

Omvar's eyes flickered with an emotion that was there and then gone. Regret, maybe. He crouched, a mountain of muscle and scale, folding his wings as if to make himself smaller. "You'll be safer with me." His voice was steady now, a low drum in my bones, but something wild burned behind it. "I walked through the city, and no one tried to stop me. Do you think they'd stop someone else? Skorai wants you back."

Skorai. Tournament Master of Ignarath. The monster's monster.

My skin went cold. No one tried to stop him. The realization trickled through my panic, chilling me to the bone. My safety here was a lie, just another thin door between me and the jaws of the world.

I dug my heels into the sleeping platform, trying to ground myself against the terror flooding every vein. "I'm not going. I can't." My voice broke, all my intended fury coming out as brittle desperation.

He sheathed his blade, the movement slow and deliberate, a statement hanging in the air between us. He raised both hands, claws tipped with blood, palms up in a gesture of surrender.

"I swear on the Forge and my honor," he said, the words thick, like a prayer, "that no harm will come to you. Not while I breathe."

A Drakarn oath. The Forge. Even I knew what that meant. Words that could not be broken.

My vision swam. I was shaking so hard my teeth clicked together. "Why would you do that?" I rasped.

He didn't answer right away. The silence stretched, heavy with his scent, smoke and ozone and something I couldn't name that called to a part of me I refused to acknowledge. His chest rose and fell. The faint, terrifying pulse of the mate-bond thrummed under my skin, ancient and wild. My body wanted to lean into that heat, to let it burn away the chill, but I recoiled from the memory of what his kind could do.

Omvar moved closer, one step, two, so careful. He stopped just out of reach, lowering his massive body to his knees to be level with me. His hand rose and hovered over my wrist. He didn't touch. I could see the tremor in him, a fight against the urge to grab me, to drag me to the safety he promised. But he didn't. He waited.

I stared at his hand. Fangs. Claws. Blood.

Fight or freeze.

I closed my eyes, trying to follow the memory of his voice. Gentle. Always gentle, even when his presence made every alarm in my body shriek.

My breathing slowed a fraction. I let my arm fall, a silent permission. He brushed his huge, warm fingers over my wrist, grounding me. Anchoring, not caging. The heat of his touch was a shock, a sudden fire that burned away some of the cold. The nightmare receded, just a little.

He leaned in, his voice a low whisper.

"If you stay here, they'll find you. Ignarath infiltrators are coming. No one else can stop them. I won't let you be taken. I swear it, on my own life."

Drakarn didn't break a Forge vow.

The stone under me felt sharp and real. The air

still stank of blood and old fear, but I could taste something else now. A sliver of hope, tangled in dread. My hands still trembled, but I didn't pull away.

He was right. No one else was coming.

This wasn't surrender. This was survival.

I met his eyes, forcing myself not to look away. "Where are we going?"

9

OMVAR

IF I LOOKED at Reika too hard, she might just disappear.

Her presence in my rooms was a fragile thing, smoke cupped in my hands. Every move I made felt like a threat that could send her scattering into nothing.

The air was thick, heavy with the rawness of recent violence and the sharp, metallic tang of blood still clinging to my scales. I'd dragged her there straight from the chaos, a warning still ringing in my throat, Ignarath blood splattered from my jaw to my wrist.

I tried to walk with care, to keep my shadow from swallowing her whole. But now, with the battered door shut behind us, the silence was a living, gnawing animal.

She hovered by the entrance, the strap of her satchel digging into her shoulder, her knuckles tense and white. I filled the small guest quarters to bursting. The stone walls, once a cool sanctuary, now pressed in, shrinking with every shallow breath she took.

Blooded warriors of Scalvaris had bigger rooms. Guest quarters weren't meant to be welcoming. It hadn't seemed small until she was in it.

Every sound drilled itself into my skull. The soft, quick scrape of Reika's breath. The brittle snap of her boots against stone as she set her bag down by the door, so careful, as if a sudden movement would shatter the uneasy peace between us. Even the faintest shuffle of her weight felt like a challenge, a test I was doomed to fail.

I was still covered in blood. A warrior always carried battle on him, but this felt different, dirtier. That she hadn't run screaming was a miracle forged in stubbornness. She anchored herself to the far wall, shoulders hunched, chin tucked, eyes darting anywhere but at me. It was instinctive. Her body screamed danger while her spirit refused to break.

My own heart thundered, too big for this space,

too loud for what passed for comfort. I kept my hands open and my movements slow, my voice softened to careful edges.

You can't force trust into a wounded thing.

Caution, stillness, a softening of the voice. These were the tools that coaxed a frightened creature close sometimes. Patience had always been a weapon in my arsenal.

But this wasn't patience. This was torment.

The memory of our kiss hung in the air, unspoken but blistering between us. I wanted to comfort her, to close the gap and crush my mouth to hers, to promise safety in the only language that felt true. But the urge itself was poison. Any wrong step, any show of strength, would make everything worse.

My want was a blade pointed at my own throat.

I scrubbed a hand down my jaw, feeling the sticky smear of drying blood. I had to get clean. I made myself small, as small as a thing like me could be.

I retreated into the narrow bathing alcove, careful to close the partition only halfway so she could see. No traps. No surprises. Just me, washing away the blood and the horror I carried on my skin.

I worked fast. Cold water bit at fresh cuts, old

battle-aches coming alive beneath my scales as I peeled off battered armor and the bloodstained tunic. Symbols of what I was, of what I'd done. The copper tang of blood chased me, refusing to be banished, but I scoured my arms clean and let the cold numb my hands.

My reflection caught me in a shard of polished obsidian above the basin: gold eyes too bright, jaw set, a monster staring back. I found a fresh shirt, black and simple, softer than what I'd worn in the field. No armor. No weapons. No claim, save the scars winding over my shoulder and chest, stories written in flesh that no amount of scrubbing could erase.

When I stepped back into the main room, Reika flinched. It was barely there, just a tightening around her eyes, a jerk of her chin. But I saw it. I felt it like a wound reopening.

I slowed everything. Breath in. Shoulders hunched, posture closed, my hands visible and empty. Part of me wanted to drop to my knees, to show her my throat, to offer every vulnerable piece of myself to prove I wasn't the monster she remembered.

That would do me no good.

"I need to go get something. Stay here." The

words dropped like hot stones, a command disguised as a plea.

Reika's head jerked up, her eyes wild. "I thought you wanted to guard me." Her tone was a snapped wire, hostile and defensive, brittle with humiliation.

A sting, but I hid it. "No one will get to you here."

The words felt empty, a lie stacked on top of all the others I'd told or kept silent. Still, she didn't move.

I forced words out past the shame. "I will return shortly." I tried to make it sound like routine, not desperation. Not an excuse to flee the heat of her panic and the acid of my own need.

She didn't answer. I lingered a moment, heavy with things unsaid, then moved into the corridor. My steps echoed down the stone, each footfall a drumbeat of guilt.

It took longer than I expected to find them.

The market had emptied while night pressed in, merchants packing away the last of their goods. The scent of honey and crisp-fried dough was nearly gone, drifting faintly above the spice of roasted meat and river moss. I bribed a vendor with a coin worth more than twice the price, careful to keep my claws in check as I carried the warm plate back to my quarters.

A dull throb started beneath my breastbone with every step. She wouldn't still be there. Of course she wouldn't. Only a fool would stay with a blood-soaked monster, even one with a Drakarn's promise stamped on his tongue. I quickened my pace, fighting the urge to run.

When I returned, Reika was right where I left her, her back to the door, arms folded, the tension in her spine gone brittle and high. Her eyes flicked to mine, searching for threat, for escape, for any sign I'd changed my mind.

I offered her the plate of honeyed sweets. I placed it on the low table between us, then retreated, giving her distance. I watched her too closely, hating myself for it.

Her hand hovered over the treats, fingers trembling as they traced the air just above the sticky shells. Her lips pressed into a thin line. I forced myself to remain still, patience a pain-bright thread pulled taut in my chest.

"How did you know I liked these?" she asked, her voice soft but edged. There was accusation in it, a challenge, as if I'd stolen a secret.

Panic flared hot in my throat. I couldn't say I'd

watched her in the market while she devoured a plate of them, eyes closed, lips shining with honey and bliss. I couldn't confess that seeing her happy, unguarded, had nearly broken me. That I'd burned the image into my memory to keep myself alive through the worst of the dark nights.

"I think everyone likes these." It was a coward's answer. The truth sat heavy just behind my teeth, a stone I couldn't spit out. Not if I wanted her to stay.

Her suspicion didn't fade. She studied the plate as if it might bite.

Slowly, Reika lifted one of the sweets. Her thumb pressed into the sticky crust, breaking the shell while honey oozed around her fingertips. She hesitated a moment longer, head bowed, then brought it to her lips.

She ate with a strange gravity, as if the morsel held a memory she needed to taste to believe it. Her tongue darted out, licking a stray drop of honey from the corner of her mouth. The gesture was so unconsciously sensual it cracked something open inside me.

The moment softened, the air less jagged. A heartbeat of quiet. She looked up, her voice distant, vulnerable in a way I'd never seen before.

"I had these for the first time in Ignarath," she

said. "I don't know why they were in my cell. Someone must have favored me." She shuddered, the memory crawling over her skin. "Whoever they were, they never called in that debt. It was the best thing I ate while I was there."

My hands curled into fists beneath the table, nails biting deep into my palms. Shame slicked the back of my tongue.

That had been me.

Months ago, hidden behind a mask of iron and discipline, I'd slipped treats past the guards when I couldn't bear her suffering another day. Too cowardly to show my face, too broken to offer more than crumbs from the feast of my guilt.

She had no idea.

I wanted to tell her. The urge to confess was a boulder at the edge of a cliff, gravity pulling it, needing only the smallest push. But I couldn't. Not now. Not if she thought there'd been a price.

"There's plenty here for both of us." She slid the plate across the table. The offering was awkward, almost shy. The gesture was clumsy, but it was hope. Her hope, extended in trembling fingers.

I took one of the sweets, careful to move slowly, non-threatening.

My fingers brushed a smear of honey from the

edge of the plate. Her eyes darted to the spot, tracking the movement, her pupils blown wide with something I didn't dare name.

We sat in silence, the tension so thick it might have been a third person in the room. The longing in me grew sharp, unbearable. A hunger not just for her body, but for the bond, for the chance to be seen as something other than her monster.

Her lips glistened. She licked the honey from her thumb, then caught me looking and snapped her gaze away. A bloom of color rose on her cheeks against pale skin.

Without thinking, she reached up, fingers hesitant, and brushed at something on my jaw. Her touch was featherlight. A single fingertip, warm and sticky, catching on a spot of honey I'd missed.

Time fractured.

I didn't breathe.

Her touch, her scent, the honey and the sweetness and the coppery thread of her fear, all tangled together, crawling over me with the crackle of lightning. Pressure built behind my ribs, a physical pain, aching for closeness, for anything to bridge the distance. I wanted to lean in, to press my face to her palm, to beg for just a second more.

"I …" I tried to speak, but my voice betrayed me, thick with longing.

She pulled away, fast and sharp, the connection snapped. Her cheeks went scarlet. Her eyes shuttered blank, her whole body drew in on itself, small and apart. She jumped up from her seat and retreated to the farthest corner of the room.

The distance yawned open again between us, as wide as the chasm between worlds. The moment was ruined, the ashes of hope drifting down around our shoulders. I was a monster. I would always be a monster.

I stared at my hands, fighting the urge to beg her to come back, to let me try again. But I'd already pressed my luck. My want was a wound I couldn't close, raw and open and exposed to the air. Reika didn't look at me. The stone walls felt smaller, the light colder.

The warmth of what might have been was already flickering out.

If I looked at her too hard, she would disappear. So I made myself look away, and waited, half alive, for something I couldn't bring myself to name.

10

REIKA

IF I THOUGHT SLEEPING in the human quarters was hard, sleeping four feet away from Omvar was a challenge my subconscious was too scared to face.

The room felt too small, and too big, both at once. Stone walls pressed in, but there was nothing to anchor myself against, just endless black and the faint, shifting yellow glow of a heat crystal that bled over everything.

It was an alien sort of dark, not the safe blanket of night from home or even the false dusk of Scalvaris's tunnels. This darkness had weight. Mass. It crawled into my chest and sat there like a boulder.

I lay curled on his too-large sleeping platform, every muscle clenched so tight it hurt. The blanket was bunched in my sweaty fists, a silky thing that was almost scratchy but radiated a low heat suffused with his scent.

Metal. Smoke. Sweat. And something deeper, something almost sweet. Not honey. Definitely not blood, though the copper-sharp ghost of it still threaded the air. A tang of sulfur clung to the humidity, coating the back of my throat.

My skin felt sticky. While my muscles screamed for rest, my mind kept gnawing on the question of why the hell I was there.

Omvar was on the floor. He'd made a nest from blankets, as if that made any difference to the way his body took over the room.

I'd tried to insist I could make a pile for myself, that I didn't need the platform, didn't deserve it, but he wouldn't hear of it. He wouldn't even look at me while he set out the bedding, just kept working silently, his hands steady, as if that could make the world make sense again.

My satchel was out of reach, flung by the door when I'd fumbled inside, half panicked, and still tasting steel and adrenaline from the brisk walk there. Not that the herbs ever really helped. Nothing did. My anchor now was this pathetic blanket, my fingers digging grooves into it with sheer force, as if I could hold myself together.

I hated how aware I was of him.

Every time he shifted, the gritty scrape of a claw against stone, or the slow, measured sound of his breathing, another jolt of panic shot through my gut. Every cell in my body was on high alert. Yet there was a kind of comfort buried under the fear. The heat of him, even from across the room, was more real than the artificial warmth of the bedding.

I closed my eyes, desperate for escape, but found no comfort in darkness. Just ghosts. The memory of him covered in blood, the fresh streaks I could still see behind my eyelids.

It wasn't just that. My mind wandered, unwanted, to the taste of honey on my tongue, the press of his mouth against mine, that desperate, wild kiss in the training caverns. The confusion rose up in me like a fever every time I thought of him.

Monster. Protector. A new hunger as sharp as a knife.

That hunger shamed me. I fought it as hard as I fought the nightmares. Harder, maybe.

I pulled the blanket tighter, balled my fists under my chin, and tried to find somewhere in my body that wasn't burning or aching or desperate. If I could just get warm, maybe. If I could trick myself into believing I was safe, even for a little while. I counted my breaths like they were steps out of hell. I repeated my makeshift mantra, the one that sometimes helped: *You are not broken. You are not broken.*

But the words were a lie, as thin as the air. Safety, always a lie.

It was only exhaustion that finally dragged me under. I let go of the world, inch by inch, and sleep took me like a thief.

Night sliced me open.

I dreamed, but the dream was a knife. The world fractured into jagged scenes. Ignarath, all screaming, the red glare of light slashing across the sand. Chains snapping against bone while voices echoed down endless corridors. I couldn't tell whose screams filled the dark, mine or someone else's.

I was running, always running, the heat of fire at my back and sharp stones cutting into my soles.

Then, in the nightmare's ugliness, he appeared.

Sometimes a shape hulking in the shadows, monstrous and nameless, hunger and agony written across a face rimmed with gold. Sometimes he was the only one not baying for my blood, his eyes fixed on mine, his hand outstretched. His claws gleamed, both a warning and a promise.

Omvar was captor and savior. The boundary blurred until it was gone. Was he the one who chased me, or the one who carved a path through the mob to reach me?

Chains and claws, comfort and cage.

Do you trust me? His voice cut through the screaming, fierce and oddly tender, a desperate drum against my bones.

But I couldn't reach him. No matter how hard I ran, the gap never closed. My throat was raw, words splintering before they could leave my mouth. Darkness closed in, suffocating.

I jerked awake with a scream caught in my throat.

My whole body was shaking, a cold sweat burning my skin while my heart rattled against my ribs like a drum demanding blood. For a long, blind moment, I had no idea where I was. The air was thick, humid, the stench of stone and blood heavy. Honey ghosted the back of my tongue. My chest heaved as I gulped the heavy air, my lungs refusing to calm.

I floundered, legs tangled in the blanket. Panic crashed over me in waves. Not a cage. Not Ignarath. Not …

I blinked, dragging myself back to the room. The dim light flickered against black, sweating walls. A shadow shifted.

Omvar was beside me, not touching, but close. His massive shape was crouched low, as if he was afraid that getting any nearer would shatter me. In the dark, his features were all sharp angles and deep shadows, his gold eyes wide and wild, but so careful as they watched me.

"Wake up," he said, his voice pitched almost gentle. "You're in Scalvaris. No harm will come to you."

He didn't touch me, and that made it easier to breathe. I stared at him, every muscle ready to snap while he waited, unmoving, as if the wrong gesture might drive me up the walls.

"Nightmare?" His knuckles grazed the edge of the platform, steady as bedrock.

I nodded, choking back the mess of words stuck in my throat. My teeth wanted to chatter, but I wouldn't let them. I forced my jaw tight, pressing my fingers into the blanket so hard my nails ached. The fear didn't drain away; it pooled, sour and bright under my skin.

He hovered there, carved from patience and worry. I saw it in the lines of his body, the way he leaned in but pulled back at the same time. His wings were pulled back so tight I almost couldn't see them.

If the world made any sense, I'd want him gone. I'd want to be alone with my ghosts. But the silence clawed at me, worse than the memory. All the old panic was still there, but loneliness was a deeper ache.

I hated this, hated how swiftly the fear could hollow me out. Yet I hated the silence more. I hated being left alone with the wreckage of my own mind.

He shifted back on his heels, like he was getting ready to go back down to the mess of blankets he was calling a bed.

My voice scraped out, a raw, ugly thing. "Can you … just, don't go. Please."

Pathetic. Weak. The words bit at my pride, but I couldn't take them back.

Omvar's eyes softened, wary and hopeful in a way that hurt to look at. He shifted his weight, climbed onto the edge of the sleeping platform. He still didn't touch me, but he was close enough that I could feel the heat radiating from his body.

I could taste his nearness. Spice and salt, sweat and something ancient that wormed under my skin, hungry and deep. My heart thrummed, uneasy. Not all fear, not quite. The comfort his presence offered warred with the terror he embodied. My body reacted anyway, soaking up the heat while my mind screamed caution.

He didn't try to bridge the gap. He just waited. His breath was a steady tide beside me, dark and rhythmic, the heaviness of it settling my frantic breathing by degrees. The silence stretched, no longer hostile. The nightmares edged away, stubborn as smoke, reluctant but receding.

With him, the dark lost some of its bite. I started to breathe again, small and slow. Each inhale brought more of his scent, less of the phantom blood and fire that haunted my skin.

My body betrayed me. I shifted closer, just enough that my shoulder brushed his.

He froze, his breath caught, as if even acknowledging the contact might ruin everything. But he didn't move away. He let me set the distance. The message in his stillness was clear: I controlled the edges of this small, dangerous peace.

Warmth gathered behind my eyes. I wanted to curl against him, to be held, to forget everything for a few careless heartbeats. I wanted so much I could barely stand it. I felt small, and sheltered, and on the brink of something terrifying.

Was I safe with him? Or was I just trading one kind of danger for another?

I shut my eyes. Heat, strength, an impossible gentleness. The memory of his body carried me a few inches farther from the dark. The bands around my chest loosened. Slowly, I let myself curl toward him. I felt the shift of the platform, the careful way he adjusted his weight, as if to support me without ever caging me in.

I pressed my forehead to the side of his arm. The scales were smooth, warm, alive. The world narrowed to the shape of him, the low hum of his breathing, the furnace heat bleeding into my bones. I felt a vast, impossible arm come around me, cautious, uncertain, and then, when I didn't jerk away, settle over my shoulders, drawing me in.

I could have cried. I didn't. I just let myself be held, for once not the only thing standing between me and the dark.

The nightmares didn't find me again. I drifted down into a silent, dreamless sleep, wrapped in heat and heavy limbs.

11

REIKA

WHERE WAS I?

That was the first shock. I woke up without a scream clawing its way up my throat, my heart not thrashing like a caged bird punching through my ribs. I just … existed. There, in the dark, warm and whole. I couldn't remember the last time I'd opened my eyes without the world bracing for me to shatter it.

Heat and shadow pressed in close, a living wall against my spine. The night came back with a serrated bite: Omvar, looming in my room, dripping blood, his voice a low command for me to come with him. Omvar, leading me through silent tunnels where his shadow was the only shield.

Omvar, giving me those honeyed donuts I'd devoured like a starving thing.

Omvar. Again and again. He was the only thread left tying me to reality.

My eyes adjusted slowly to the yellow creep of the heat crystal overhead. Its glow limped across stone walls and ragged textiles, painting Omvar's room in bruised light. The air was thick, heavy with his scent and the ghost of copper. Blood, dried and baked into the seams between stone and flesh. The platform was a nest of tangled blankets, and it radiated the kind of warmth you could almost mistake for safety.

The word "safety" surfaced, and my brain spat it up like poison. It tasted foreign, unfamiliar, almost sweet. The idea of it curled in my gut.

His arm was thrown over my waist. Its rough scales were hard and smooth in alternating lines against my skin. His wing was a near-weightless canopy draped over us both—yet it felt like the most solid thing I'd ever known.

I lay frozen, my chest tight, my awareness a live wire stretched between every point where his body held me. My fingers trembled against his wrist, twitching along the ridges that ran over sinew and scale. I half expected him to jolt awake and make me explain myself. Half dared, stupidly, stubbornly, to believe this was allowed. That I could want this, want him, for even a moment.

With the edge of my mind, I poked at the feeling, bracing for it to bite back. Wanting had always been dangerous. Maybe deadly. But here, now, nothing snapped or snarled. Nothing chased me down for daring. Just Omvar, a furnace all around me, breathing slow and deep like he could sleep through a cave-in. His heat was animal, alien, but it soothed the frayed edges of old panic.

Shouldn't I be terrified?

Shouldn't I run?

The instinct was there, a raw, twitchy thing, but something new was drowning it. Hunger. A wild ache in the hollow beneath my heart. I wanted to press closer. To see if the warmth I felt was real.

I let my fingertips brush over his wrist, mapping the intricate patterns of scales with a featherlight touch. They felt impossibly smooth, nothing like the rough, scabbed hands of slavers.

No.

This was a different kind of danger. Tempting. Inviting. Making promises I wasn't sure my body was ready to test.

Slowly, uncertainly, I trailed my fingers up,

letting them glide over the corded muscle of his forearm. Omvar didn't move. Just a steady mountain of heat, alive but untouchable. I inched higher, over the rise of his elbow, the soft indentation where crimson scales faded to something almost like blush. I kept going, my heart pounding a frantic rhythm in my ears, drunk on the audacity of it. Wanting more. Wanting to know every inch of what the world said I should fear.

He began to stir. A ripple of movement went through him as his hand twitched, claws flexing just enough to send a warning through my skin. I jerked my hand back, guilt flooding me, sick with the certainty I'd broken some fragile peace.

But his voice came, sleep-rough, rumbling from the shadows into the cradle of space he'd made for me. "You don't have to stop."

He didn't pull his wing away. If anything, it pressed closer, a pocket of warmth that felt like a world inside his world. I swallowed, the words thick and sweet as honey on my tongue.

I knew I shouldn't.

Just looking at him most days made me shake, and not in a way I liked to admit. But there, cocooned in the impossible, I was weightless. Braver than I had any right to be.

My fingers kept wandering—this time with more certainty—skating up his forearm to his bicep. It was hard as weapon-forged steel but underlaid with a living heat that pulsed against my palm. My hand trailed along the curve of his chest, finding the faint rises and valleys of old scars, the texture as familiar as my own nightmares. He grunted, a low, involuntary sound sharp enough to make me freeze.

He didn't flinch. "Don't stop," he rumbled, softer this time, as if he was afraid I'd vanish if he spoke too loudly.

His encouragement went off in my veins like a shot of something dangerous and heady. I let my hand drift farther, mapping the heat, the dizzying landscape of his anatomy. Over the dips of old wounds, over the place where his scales faded to something softer above his heart. His chest rose and fell, his breath stuttering. I could feel it, a trembling under the surface, a coil of pleasure and tension, both vulnerable and terrifying.

His body wasn't human. It wasn't safe. But it wasn't a threat, not right now.

My hand slipped lower, curiosity untethered from shame. I found the ridged lines of his belly, the plates of scale giving way to something silkier, stranger. My heart hammered. I half thought he'd stop me, but he stayed almost painfully still, his chest heaving, the only sign I wasn't dreaming this.

I let my hand trace the instinctual line down, below his waist, toward the forbidden. I told myself I was only curious, only cataloging the alien. But the ache between my thighs told a different story.

My fingers found slickness, hot and silken under my touch.

His cock.

I should have recoiled. I should have curled away. Instead, I pressed in, exploring the strange anatomy. Scales at the base gave way to thick, ridged flesh, with thicker veins pulsing beneath the skin.

I curled my hand around him. Slick with his own fluid, hot and alive, the tip was crowned by a moving, fleshy lip that was almost like a tongue, twitching as I pressed my thumb along its seam. The head was wider than any human I'd known.

And a scent rose up between us, alien but magnetic: copper, smoke, a sweetness that made my mouth water and my core clench.

A part of me wanted to dive in and taste him. I was going absolutely fucking insane.

Omvar sucked in a shuddering breath. His hips

jerked, a subtle but unmistakable movement. He was hard. For me.

I froze, shame and wonder warring for dominance. I couldn't see his face, not in this dim light, but I could hear the way his breathing fractured, a guttural, helpless note buried under restraint. He tried to roll away, but my grip tightened. I didn't want him to move. I wanted ...+

god, I wanted this. The feeling scared me. It lit me up and unmade me all at once.

"You don't have to," I said, the words tumbling out, echoing his earlier. It shocked me how much I meant them. I wanted him to know I was choosing this. Just this once. Choosing him.

How long had it been since I'd let myself want something that wasn't survival?

He was still, as if waiting for some final, invisible permission. I gave it with my hands. I stroked him, slow at first, learning his body by feel.

The slickness, the way that lip flexed and curled with every pass of my fingers, the way the scent deepened and thickened as his pleasure built. I pumped my hand, gentle at first, then harder, chasing the sound of his breath, the stuttering grunts and soft gasps that made heat curl low in my belly.

His hand covered mine, huge and careful, his claws just barely pricking the spaces between my fingers. The contact sent sparks through every nerve ending, a delicious, sharp brightness. I liked it. I liked the danger, the way he could break me and chose not to.

He jerked once, a sharp gasp on his lips, and then his body shuddered, a pulse of wet heat spilling through my grip. He came in my hand, the fluid flooding my palm, the scent of him thick and wild, marking the air between us. The slick, musky heat of him coated my skin. It was both alien and achingly intimate.

He faltered, his body trembling against mine. For a moment, all I could hear was the thundering of his heart, loud and uneven against my back. I should have felt powerful. In control. Remaking my body as mine, not just a cage of trauma. Instead, I felt everything at once: arousal and fear, grief and want, all twisting together like molten metal.

Omvar leaned in closer, careful, reverent, his breath a hot whisper at my ear. "Let me give you this, *thravena*."

The word was an invocation, hungry and gentle. I felt it in my bones.

A thousand reasons to say no avalanched

through my mind. What if I froze? What if the pleasure tipped into panic? What if I couldn't stop once I started? What if I needed this more than I wanted to admit? But the ache was bigger. I wanted to feel something that wasn't fear.

I nodded. Maybe I whispered yes. Maybe I just offered my body, trembling and raw, to the moment.

He moved slowly, as if I might shatter. His hand brushed my hip, his claws tracing a whisper-light path down my thigh. He guided me onto my back, his wing and arms caging me in a world apart from everything else. He paused, his breath warm against my belly, waiting for the flinch that would end this.

Instead, I reached for him. I threaded shaking fingers through the coarse silk of his hair, giving him permission with the only language I knew.

He lowered his head. The first touch of his mouth at my inner thigh was so gentle it almost undid me. His tongue, long and impossibly agile, tasted the inside of my knee, painting a slow, burning line up to where I ached for him. Every nerve lit up, confusion and pleasure winding together until I couldn't tell them apart.

He licked up, then down, circling, teasing, drinking in the shudders that racked my body.

When his mouth found me, truly found me, I

bucked, a strangled gasp tearing from my throat. He licked me open, his mouth hot and wet, his tongue working in slow, deliberate strokes. He was infinitely careful, reading every twitch and gasp, flooding me with warmth and the sharp scorch-pain of wanting more.

I couldn't see him. I could only feel. His mouth, his tongue, the strange, careful pressure as he worshipped me, mapping every inch with a devotion that felt like hunger. His breath came hot against my skin. His hands bracketed my hips, holding me steady but never trapping me.

The pleasure built slow, then faster, wound tight as a wire ready to snap. I let myself want, letting the pleasure unfurl in waves, trembling through me, knocking loose memories I'd locked away. Pain and humiliation, but also the faint ghost of being chosen.

Tears prickled behind my eyes, hot and unshed.

You are not broken, I repeated, my makeshift mantra. *You are not broken.* But maybe I was. Maybe that was all right.

He found a rhythm that drove me wild, his tongue flicking, his mouth sucking, closing around me. I let go, hips canting up, a sob torn loose by pure sensation.

My orgasm hit with the force of a landslide, overwhelming, blinding, cathartic. It was a flood of feeling that wrenched a scream from my lips. I shook, nerves sparking, my hands clutching at his hair like an anchor. For a second, I was lost, adrift in pleasure tangled with old pain. Everything tilted and broke and reformed.

Omvar held me through it, his arms bracketing my body, his mouth gentling as I rode out the aftershocks. He murmured something I didn't understand, words rough and calming, his voice a steady drum in the storm. I let myself collapse, spent and shaking, into his embrace, too wrung out to move or speak.

I floated, tucked against his chest, caught between satisfaction and confusion. The air was heavy with his scent, with the ghost of honey on my tongue and the copper of old blood. My body thrummed, every muscle slack, every nerve alive.

I fixated on the strangeness of my own craving, the terror and want tangled too deep to unpick. Was this healing? Or was it just another surrender to something bigger than me, something that might own me if I let it?

Clinging to him in the silence, the question

burned inside me. I didn't know if safety was a lie. I only knew I wanted to stay.

MY MATE SMELLED of honey and my own release.

The scent clung to me. Her sweetness mingled with the musk of what we had done, soaking into the nest of blankets until I was sure it marked me as deeply as any scar. It was an impossible claim, and it seeped into every breath I took.

I watched her sleep, a tangle of bare limbs and shadowed hair, her body pressed close to where I sprawled on my side. In the hush of my quarters, with only the pulse of the heat crystal breaking the dark, a deep, possessive satisfaction settled hot and heavy in my gut.

This night wasn't something I ever believed I'd have. Not truly.

Even now, with her heartbeat a steady thrum

against my ribs and her scent a brand on my skin, I half expected to wake and find the world unchanged. Her curled away from me, my own desperation a hungry, unspent thing, the city's suspicions a poison thickening in the air. But she was here. She chose this. For a few hours, there was no one else. The taste of her was still a ghost on my tongue, and I was a different male for it.

One taste would never be enough.

Lying beside her was its own kind of torture. She curled in close, trusting in her sleep, her thigh thrown over mine and her cheek pressed against my shoulder, as if she believed I could keep her nightmares at bay just by existing. I ran a careful hand down the fragile arch of her spine, memorizing the specific heat of her skin, the small shivers in her muscles as she drifted deeper into dreams.

I wanted more. Always more. It was a hunger that never quit gnawing at me, an animal need to protect, to claim, to make her body answer to mine until I could finally believe this was real.

The city was silent on the other side of the stone, but my nerves were scraped raw, twitching. My mind scoured every shadow for threats, even as I tried to drown myself in her warmth. Every patch of darkness felt too deep. Every whisper of movement beyond these walls was a claw scraping against my instincts.

Thravena. She was mine. Mine to guard. Mine to keep safe.

Her breath hitched, that soft sigh that nearly undid me. My hand stilled on her back, not daring to break the spell. But the world outside pressed in, and the need to hunt, to eliminate what would hurt her, spiked until my muscles burned with it. I couldn't rest. Couldn't close my eyes and pretend the threat was gone just because she was in my arms. Ignarath's tendrils were out there, slithering through the city's veins, watching and waiting.

I pulled myself away, the movement slow, careful not to wake her. The blankets shifted, and for a single, sharp heartbeat, I just breathed her in. The honeyed sweetness, the ghost of fear, the echo of pleasure.

I had to let it go.

Easing out of the bed, my claws made only the faintest scrape on the stone. She mumbled something, rolling into the hollow I left behind, the loss of my heat making her curl tighter. I pulled a blanket higher over her shoulder, a useless gesture that couldn't shield her from anything. Only I could do that now.

The moment the door sealed behind me, the comfort of her presence flickered out, replaced by the oppressive stillness of Scalvaris before dawn. I moved through the tunnels with the practiced silence of a predator, my senses honed to a razor's edge. The city breathed with a slow, suffocating rhythm, the air thick with tension. Cool stone underfoot was slick with the ever-present dampness of this place. In the walls, heat crystals bled a dim, yellow light that cast monstrous, dancing shadows at every turn.

These corridors sprawled, labyrinthine, their silence a trap. I prowled a familiar patrol route where every corner was mapped in my muscle memory, every alcove a place where an enemy could lurk. A place where a scent might cling. Where Ignarath infiltrators might slip in and vanish. My nostrils flared, dragging in the city's thick, acrid air, searching for a hint of foreign scales or the sharp, metallic tang of blood.

Nothing.

A trace of burnt musk at a crossroads was just old fear, an echo from my own skin. A faint scuff of claw on stone, but it was only a fledgling, already gone. I stalked deeper, the city's pulse never quickening, only the hush growing heavier, pressing against my skull like a physical weight. The silence was suffocating, worse than any cry in the dark. No alarms. No foreign scent. No excuse to spill blood and call it justice.

I hated it. Hated that the only thing I could do was look, circle, and snarl at shadows. Was that all I was? An outcast with nothing to offer but nightmares and the memory of violence?

I circled back, each empty corridor feeding a fresh hunger for a fight that couldn't be satisfied. The threat was still out there, coiled in every shadow. I found nothing. No Ignarath agent, no reason to strike. Just the city locked down tight, holding its breath.

Returning to my quarters, every bone in my body vibrated with the effort not to smash something just to prove I was still alive. Reika slept on, curled so tightly in the tangle of blankets it looked like she was trying to disappear. I sat on the edge of the bed and watched her chest rise and fall, my hands planted between my knees. I wanted to join her, to let exhaustion finally swallow me, but I couldn't. Couldn't let myself go soft. Not when one wrong moment meant she'd be gone.

I sat vigil. Waiting for the world to break.

Hours later, a sharp rap at the door cracked the

heavy hush of the room. I rose, my blood a hot surge in my veins, my jaw set. That kind of knock signaled a summons. I should've expected it. After yesterday, after volunteering for duty then vanishing and stalking the tunnels dripping Ignarath blood, I was already drawing too many eyes.

I eased the door open, careful not to completely block the view of the bed. A runner handed me a piece of paper stamped with Darrokar's seal. The Blade Council wanted a word.

Perfect. Political theater before breakfast.

Reika stirred, blinking up at me with cautious eyes. Bleary, soft, and instantly wary. The sight speared something vital in my chest.

"Darrokar wants to talk," I told her, my voice low. "You'll be safe here while I'm gone."

She propped herself up on one elbow. "Are you going to leave me locked up in your rooms every day?" Her tone was brittle, somewhere between a tease and an accusation, the real question hiding just underneath.

I hesitated. Did she want freedom? Or did she want me to stay? My own instincts screamed to keep her there, locked away from the world, but I'd seen her broken by cages too many times.

"Would you like to go to the human quarters?" I

forced my voice to stay gentle, though it grated against my possessive need. "If others are there and I post a guard, it could be safe." The thought of anyone else watching her made bile rise in my throat.

She'd been caged enough.

Her eyes flicked away. "I'll be okay." A lie, told for both our sakes.

We stood in that awful, awkward silence, the air thick with things we would not say. I was torn between the urge to reach for her and the certainty that if I did, I would shatter something fragile between us.

Our gazes caught. I didn't dare press a kiss to her temple, didn't trust myself to touch her without taking more. In the end, I just nodded and turned, walking out with her scent burning a path down my spine.

The city swallowed me. The tunnels were warmer now, the light flickering with the first hints of day. I made my way to the Blade Council chamber, a vast space carved from volcanic rock where every step echoed with the weight of tradition and ancient violence. Its heavy doors stood open, and the heat crystals set deep in the walls cast long lines of light like drawn swords.

Inside, the council waited.

Darrokar was a mountain of obsidian scales and coiled authority, his massive form radiating command even at rest. Khorlar, gray-scaled and blunt as ever, stood with arms crossed, watching me with unreadable eyes. Nyx lounged nearby, his posture deceptively casual, but his gaze was sharp enough to flay a lesser warrior.

I squared my shoulders and crossed to the center of the floor, the battered insignia of Scalvaris tight around my arm, the only marker of my precarious belonging. The silence in the chamber was a physical thing, every heartbeat a drum against my ribs.

Darrokar's voice was cold steel. "You brought a war to my city, Ignarath." It wasn't an accusation, just a statement of fact as heavy as a judgment.

"The war was coming whether I lived here or not," I said, my voice a growl made careful by effort. My claws flexed at my sides.

Khorlar's jaw worked, the ripple of suspicion and resentment never quite leaving his face. Nyx watched, a flicker of sharp curiosity under all that practiced indifference.

Darrokar's gaze pinned me, blade sharp. "Why

now? What does Skorai want? What makes these humans worth the risk?"

My chest tightened. I thought of Reika in her cage, of the way Skorai made a sport of breaking spirits. Of how he saw all things as property, as challenges to his supremacy.

"Skorai's pride is wounded," I said, spitting the words. I hated how close they twisted to the truth of my own failings. "He sees the escaped humans as stolen. As challenges to his power. He doesn't care who bleeds, so long as he proves he cannot be defied."

"Why would he risk open conflict for so few?" Nyx asked, his voice smooth as oil, his tail flicking with interest.

I faced them, rage simmering just under the surface of my skin. "To make an example. To terrify the rest. To remind us all that the cages aren't ever empty." Their questions were like prodding at old wounds, but I forced the words out, each one a blade.

The council circled me with words, with tactics and consequences. They spoke of risks and alliances as if this were a game of pieces, not flesh and blood. My teeth ached with the need to roar.

"There are others," I cut in, my voice dropping

to a low, rolling threat. "Humans still in Ignarath. In the cages." I met Darrokar's stare, holding it with the weight of everything I had lost. "Will you send a force? Will you bring them back?"

He had his own human mate. If he would do it for nothing else, he should do it for her.

Darrokar's jaw tightened, a crack in the mask of his authority. Whatever he felt, he didn't show it. "An assault on Ignarath is not a decision to be made lightly. Escalation would be unavoidable. We must have patience."

The word burned, useless as water on hot stone. Patience. Politics. Words. All useless.

I thought of Reika, of what she had suffered, of the others still enduring it. My fists clenched, claws digging hard enough to draw blood from my palms. I didn't know how I could save them, but I knew something had to be done. I would not stand by while this city debated itself into paralysis. Not again.

I left the chamber with their caution thick as oil in the air and my rage coiling ever tighter in my chest, a promise echoing in my bones.

I would not fail her again.

The hunt wasn't over.

Not until every shadow was burned away.

TWO DAYS of breathing Omvar's air, sleeping in his bed, eating the food he brought me like some prized pet.

I told myself this was protection. A measure of safety. But the line between protection and captivity was blurring, the stone walls of his quarters transforming from a shield into a cage.

A comfortable one, yes, lined with soft blankets that smelled of him, a scent that promised no harm could reach me there. But it was a cage all the same.

Was I truly safe, or just hidden away?

Shadows pooled in the corners of the room, stretching and shrinking with my every move, a reminder that there were no windows and only one door. Only the oppressive warmth pressing in and the scent of Drakarn, a mix of smoke, hot metal, and a sweetness that now clung to my skin.

I pulled the blanket tighter around my shoulders, his scent sinking into me. It was invasive, persistent. My pulse tripped every time I breathed it in. There was a comfort there, a feeling so potent it felt like a betrayal of something I couldn't name.

I hated how I knew he was near before I saw him, how the ache in my chest quieted at the sound of his heavy footsteps outside. I hated how, despite everything, my body settled when I knew he was close.

What did that make me? Pet, prisoner? Both? Maybe neither. Maybe just a survivor who'd gotten too used to hiding in caves.

This wasn't Ignarath. Omvar kept his distance, mostly. Except for those smoldering looks he shot me when he thought I wasn't watching. There hadn't been a repeat of that first night.

Thankfully.

Terribly.

The memory was a constant, looping thing I swore I'd ignore. His arms closing around me, the surprising heat of his scales under my palms, the way his mouth had found me, both hungry and careful at once. I'd gone soft in his hold, surrendered to a touch I thought would break me. I'd wanted it. Even with the fear coiling in my gut like a snake, I'd wanted to forget why I should be afraid.

But the memory always soured. I could feel my own independence slipping, replaced by a need that scared me more than any nightmare.

With Omvar, I didn't have to be strong. I didn't have to do anything but exist. It was a terrifying relief. Needing someone so badly always ended in pain. I'd fought too hard to survive just to trade one keeper for another.

In my first weeks there, every step outside my rooms had ended with me screaming, clawing at walls, begging for a safety that didn't exist. I had come so far. I almost didn't shake when I walked alone now. Almost.

But the comfort of this room called to me, dark and forbidden. It would be so easy to get used to this, to let myself disappear behind the broad back and wings of my Drakarn protector.

They called him the Beast in Ignarath. Here, he was my beast.

But no matter how good the blanket felt, I

couldn't pretend it was freedom. I couldn't let him hold me prisoner, not even if I was willing.

My tongue felt thick, my pulse a frantic drum against my ribs. I could hear him moving in the outer alcove, his steps slow and careful. Giving me space. As if space wasn't just another kind of cage.

I shoved the blanket away. The sudden loss of warmth made my skin tighten. I forced myself to walk into the main room, arms wrapped around my middle as if holding myself together. Omvar stood half in shadow, his gold eyes tracking my every move. A tension hung in the air, so fragile that a single loud word might shatter it.

My throat was dry. "I can't just stay here." The words came out as a crackle of sound.

He went utterly still, every muscle locking into place. "What?"

Was I being stupid? Was I about to destroy the only scrap of comfort I'd found in months?

My voice came out sharper this time, honed by a fear I refused to show. "I can't hide away forever. Have you heard anything about the Ignarath? Is there any news?"

His posture snapped rigid, wings clamping tight to his back. The guard went up so fast it was like a physical blow, erasing the softness he'd held just a moment before. He watched me with a wariness that made my skin crawl and my heart ache.

I felt like I was back in the arena, exposed under a thousand hostile eyes, every word a gamble.

"You came for me like some monster," I blurted, my words harsh and uneven. "You dragged me away. I can't … I just …" I swallowed against a mouth gone dry as desert sand. "I need the truth."

He didn't flinch. His voice was a low rumble, final. "The threat is real. I killed one, and we captured two. Your name was mentioned. Skorai wants you back."

A cold fist squeezed deep in my gut, stealing my breath. "But why?" I pressed, even though part of me already knew. I needed to hear it from him, from someone who wasn't in the business of selling hope.

His tail twitched, the only sign of his agitation. "Slaves who escape Ignarath are captured and returned. Anyone who assists them is executed or enslaved themselves. Ignarath has gone to war for less. That a human escaped? It is an insult almost beyond bearing. If he cannot have you back, he will kill you."

The words struck like a slap. I stood there, arms wrapped tight around myself, as he recounted the interrogation, his voice flat. The assassins were specialized killers, sent directly by Skorai. Their orders were simple: target escapees, send a message. My name, spat out in that guttural Ignarath snarl, made it all real.

Each detail made the walls close in, the air growing thick and suffocating. My mind spun through faces: Kinsley, Kira, Vega. "What about Kinsley?" I demanded. "Or the others who are still there? That envoy came here to steal humans. Are we all in danger?"

His gaze flickered for just a second. A muscle jumped in his jaw, his eyes darting away as if looking at me too long might break something between us. I locked onto that tiny crack, hope and fury a volatile mix in my chest.

"Well?" My voice rose, sharp as shattered glass. "Are they safe?"

A silence followed, heavier than before. He looked down, working his jaw, grinding the words before he let them out. When his eyes finally met mine, there was nothing left in his face but raw, brutal honesty. No monster. No protector. Just him.

"I don't know," he said, his voice flat and final. "You are the only one in this damned city that I care about."

It landed like a punch to the gut. I swayed, caught between the urge to lash out and the urge to collapse into him. The air crackled, the weight of his confession pressing on me from all sides.

Only me.

How could that be true?

THE CONFESSION HUNG in the air between us, heavy and suffocating.

You are the only one.

It wasn't sweet. It was obsession. Possession. Another name for a chain, and the air in his quarters suddenly felt too thin to breathe. The stone walls pressed in, a solid weight against my ribs until my lungs ached with the effort of fighting them.

What the fuck had I gotten myself into?

Claustrophobia, sharp and familiar, clawed its way up my throat. I scrambled back, my feet shuffling desperately on stone to put distance between myself and the heat rolling off his body.

Away from the crushing weight of his confession.

"I have to get out of here." The words were a ragged gasp. If I stayed another second, I might just crumble into dust.

A wound opened in his gold eyes, a flicker of pain that punched me in the gut. His hands, which had been hanging loose at his sides, curled into fists, the knuckles straining, white as if he were physically stopping himself from reaching for me. He took a single, predatory step forward.

"It's not safe." His voice was a low rumble, an attempt at reason that still vibrated with command.

"Nothing is fucking safe!" The words tore from me, sharp and brittle. "Don't you get that? Are you going to keep me here like some prized pet? Like one of them?"

My accusation struck him harder than a physical blow. The war on his face was stark, a battle between the possessive beast that wanted to cage me and the male who was bleeding from the wounds my words inflicted. He lowered his head, a gesture of submission so utterly alien to his nature that it left me breathless all over again. Then, he stepped aside, clearing the path to the door.

An open cage.

I bolted.

The path to the river was a blur of stone and

shadow. I couldn't go back to my usual spot, the memory of the acolytes and their slick, hateful voices tainting it forever. But the banks were vast.

I found a new place, a small alcove carved into the rock face that felt almost private, almost hidden. The air was colder there, cutting through the thin fabric of my shirt with a clean, sharp bite.

I sank to the ground. My knees came up to my chest, my satchel resting uselessly at my side.

His words replayed in my head. *You are the only one.*

A terrifying restriction and a dangerously seductive promise. It was a blanket woven from fire and steel, offering warmth that would either protect me or burn me alive. I replayed the feel of his arms, the terrifying gentleness that was at war with the monster I knew his kind could be.

He was a cage I might actually want to stay in, and that thought scared me more than Ignarath's whips.

A shadow was the only warning I got.

Vyne landed without a sound. Silent. Effortless. His green scales seemed to absorb the light of the cavern, making him a void in the shape of a Drakarn. He didn't look at me. He just stood sentinel several feet away, his powerful presence an unspoken statement.

Omvar's long, protective shadow.

Moments later, a softer sound. Selene. She approached not as a warrior, but as a friend, her steps careful on the uneven stone. She sat beside me, leaving a thoughtful sliver of space between us, a quiet offering of solidarity that I hadn't realized I was starving for. The steady rush of the river filled the silence until the frantic trembling in my limbs began to subside.

"Did he send you?" I whispered. Anything louder felt like a violation of the fragile peace.

Selene nodded, her gaze kind but unnervingly clear. "He's worried." She paused, letting the words settle. "What are you running from, Reika? Ignarath? Or him?"

The question landed hard, knocking the air from my lungs. The shame of it twisted through me like jagged glass. I wanted to scream that I was running from the monsters, from the memories, from the scent of blood and the clang of cage doors. But it wasn't the whole truth. It wasn't even close.

My throat felt tight. "I don't know what I want." It was the most honest thing I had said in months.

"Don't you?" Selene's voice was soft, but it held no pity, only a quiet challenge. "I think there's a big part of you that isn't scared. A part that's tired of being a victim."

I squeezed my eyes shut, the truth of her words a brand against my heart. Running hadn't given me peace. It had just left me exhausted and alone, chasing a phantom of safety that I could never catch. I could keep running until I faded into nothing.

Or I could turn and face the one thing that scared me more than any monster.

Hope.

"I'm so tired of being fucking weak," I finally whispered, the admission cracking something open deep inside me. I looked up, meeting Selene's steady gaze.

A small, proud smile touched her lips before she gave me a sharp nod of encouragement. She stood, a fluid motion of grace and strength, and signaled to the silent shadow that was Vyne. She stepped into his arms, and he wrapped his wings around her, launching them both into the air.

I stood, my legs shaking but holding me up. I took a deep breath of the cold, clean air, letting it fill my lungs, letting it scour the last of the panic from my blood. I didn't know exactly what I was walking toward.

A cage or a sanctuary. A beast or a savior.

But I knew, deep in my bones, that I was done running.

15

OMVAR

I'D LOST HER.

The fact settled with the quiet, grinding finality of a tomb sealing shut. After every broken vow, every bloody mile, I'd lost her anyway. I sat hunched in the cold hollow of my quarters, my back braced against the wall.

The air was thick with the stink of my own failure. Above, a heat crystal sputtered a sickly yellow light, its glow too weak to push the darkness from the corners of the room. Ignarath's shadow circled closer with every passing hour, a storm on the horizon with its claws already outstretched for my throat.

She was gone. I hadn't been enough.

The truth was a crushing weight. All the rage I'd carried from the desert, every righteous snarl, had only left me caged here. I was alone except for the ghost of her scent on the air. The mate-bond burned in my chest, a hot, twisting ache that stole my breath, but it didn't matter.

If she didn't want me, didn't want this, then no bond could force her to stay.

But that didn't mean I would stop protecting her. It only took a moment to send a runner to Vyne with the details, stripped of all pleading. If I knew her—and despite it all, I thought I did—she would go to the river.

Vyne knew the city's veins, and he was mated to Selene, the only healer I trusted with Reika's soul. If anyone could help her, it was them.

If anyone deserved to, it wasn't me.

I forced myself to my feet. Every muscle coiled tight with the urge to destroy something, to rend stone and flesh until this poison of helplessness had somewhere to go. But there was nowhere left to spend it. The beast I'd kept caged for so long stirred under my ribs, ready to strike anything that came too close. Except there was nothing left worth striking.

Just the silence.

Hours of silence. Pacing. And something I refused to call fear.

I wasn't going to see her again.

Except she was there. Standing in the rough-hewn arch of my doorway like vengeance made flesh.

The door scraped open, and she slipped inside. She wasn't small. She wasn't cowering. The air in the room changed, growing heavy and charged, every shadow holding its breath. She crossed her arms, a challenge carved from stone and unshakable will, the kind of force that survives a hell like Ignarath and every torment that comes after.

I was a statue frozen by pain. I didn't dare speak, didn't dare move. The bond between us snapped inside me, a visceral tug that seized my heart and groin, a thrum that followed the defiant line of her body. It was more wound than gift. Painful. Hungry.

With a low groan, the door shut behind her. My entire world shrank to her silhouette against the gloom. The space between us vibrated with unspoken things. My heart hammered in my ribs, my scales prickling with every breath she took.

She took a step deeper into the room. I watched

the tension in her shoulders, the white-knuckled grip of her hands on her arms, the hard set of her jaw.

Fragile control hung over her like a thread stretched to its breaking point. Her eyes, wide and dark and bruised with exhaustion, found mine and held me pinned. I knew that look. It was a challenge. And it was a plea.

"Those sweets …," she started, her voice a low, scraped sound that was still somehow steady. She shook her head sharply, as if trying to dislodge something soft. Then she changed her question.

"What's so special about me?"

It was a battering ram to my chest. How could I explain? How could I tell her about the bond, about the way her name burned on my tongue like a prayer that would only drive her away? If I told her the truth, would she run again? Run for good? My heart spasmed at the thought, a terrible kick of terror and hope.

She stared at me, waiting. The silence stretched until it was nearly painful.

"Answer me." Her voice cut like a blade.

I had to give her something. Anything but the whole, unbearable truth.

"I saw you," I forced out, the words tasting like

ash. "Hundreds of people in the arena, but it was just you."

Her mouth twisted. "You're talking about Ignarath."

It was the place that bound us. That haunted us.

"When your ship crashed, Skorai had his claws so deep in me I thought I'd never get out. I was his pet champion. The monster on his leash. And I accepted that." My own confession was poison, admitting I'd survived by being cruel, by turning a blind eye. "Until I saw you. I couldn't *do* anything. If I'd shown you the tiniest scrap of favor, he would have used it to hurt you. Or worse, given you to me."

Her eyes flashed. "So you just left me to suffer?"

Shame, hot and thick, rose in my throat. My claws bit into my palms. "I did what I could to protect you."

I made myself meet her gaze, laying out the truth stone by stone, each admission worse than the last. "Extra food, when I could get it. Cleaner water. I made sure the worst of the guards, the ones who hurt for sport, never worked your corridor again. I took two of them out. Made it look like a drunken brawl." My voice had gone flat, defensive. Empty. She'd been locked in a cage, and all I could offer was cleaner water and a sliver of chance. "I created an opening in the patrols. I was coming to get you out."

I had to move, to pace, or I might explode with the emotion simmering underneath.

"I should have torn down the walls of that pit to reach you. And I didn't. For that, I have no excuse."

She sucked a breath through her teeth. I watched understanding flicker in her eyes.

The unlocked door, the food, the moments of calm she knew she couldn't trust in that place. Every tiny mercy, revealed. The ghost in the dark, the one she'd never seen, now stood before her as flesh and scale and shame.

She took a shaky step closer. Her courage was a living thing in the curl of her hands, the rigid set of her jaw.

"But why?" The question was a whisper, wrecked and fierce, yet it echoed around the bare chamber as if the stone itself demanded an answer. "Why risk everything?"

The question ripped me open.

Because you are my mate. Because you are the only hope I have left.

But the words were a chain. Sacred to my kind, but for her, just another cage.

I couldn't stop myself from taking a half step forward, closing the distance. I kept my hands open, palms out. Surrender was written in every line of my monstrous form. There was nothing left but the truth.

"Because you are my mate," I said.

The word rang in the air like a struck bell. Sacred. Damning. Everything I'd tried not to say.

She flinched, a tremor that ran through her as if the word itself were a brand searing her skin.

I struggled to explain, my voice raw. "It's not just biology. It's a pull. A certainty in my blood. I knew you the moment I saw you, the first time I caught your scent in that pit. It's why I defected. Why I tracked you here. It's the reason I would burn this city to nothing to keep you safe."

I let her see it all: the desperation, the hunger, the shame.

"I would have died in Ignarath, but I couldn't let Skorai have you. So I watched. I waited. I did what little I could. It was never enough."

I looked at her then, really looked, the bond a line of acid under my scales. "I gave you the tools. The unlocked door. I gave you everything I could. If you want my life, you can have it."

I braced for the blow.

She choked on a sound, her eyes glossing over, tears brimming but not yet falling. Her body trembled, caught between reaching for me and recoiling. I saw it all in her face. Shock, disbelief, old wounds cracking open, and something helpless and incandescent fought its way out.

"So this is all just … biological imperative?"

Something snapped inside me. "No. Never. Not just that."

My denial came out as a ragged snarl. I let every defense I had fall at her feet. "You are not a compulsion. You are not just fate. I would choose you. In any world, any body, any life. It's you. It has always been you."

She took a step, then another, until she stood directly before me. The space between us was charged, the heat a living thing. My chest ached with a pain so sharp I thought it might split wide open.

Her hands lifted, trembling, and hung in the air between us. Not a caress, not a refusal. Her face was a ruin of pain and hope, the ghost of her old life warring with the burning edge of something new.

I remained perfectly still. Open. Waiting. I would not touch her until she chose. I would not be her monster. Not now.

She was the one who moved.

Her hands lifted, hovering in the air between us. Not to push me away. Not to pull me closer. Just … there. A question.

One I couldn't answer alone.

I WAS HIS MATE.

His mate.

Some sick, cosmic joke, right? My body should have been screaming to run. I should have been sprinting for the door, back toward the river, clawing my way through six tons of rock just to escape the ancient, brutal certainty in his voice.

But I didn't. Not even close.

My hands were steady as I lifted them. I uncurled my stiff fingers one by one. The tension that had become my body's default setting, the constant readiness to fight or flee, finally just … unspooled.

I traced the angle of his jaw, slow, greedy, memorizing the texture of scales beneath my fingertips. They were surprisingly smooth, a mosaic of hard, living warmth. Each one bowed around the line of bone, a specific, textured heat that radiated into my palm.

He was all edges and ridges, a creature forged for battle, but I wasn't afraid.

My fingers ventured upward, skimming over a scar that split the scales, a raised seam of memory. He could have snapped that jaw shut, could have drawn blood in a blink, but he held perfectly still.

A mountain, letting me touch him, letting me claim every part I dared.

His eyes shut, lashes a dark, thick fringe against red skin. Vulnerable. Reverent. For once, the monster from my nightmares looked like a man stripped of his armor, letting me see the monumental cost of his surrender.

For a long, breathless stretch, I just watched him, letting the moment settle, letting myself drown in the impossible security of it. The stone walls, once a cage, were now a sanctuary. It pressed in close, holding me up instead of burying me.

I wanted him.

The truth crashed over me, raw and scorching as magma. I wanted him to claim me. I wanted the way his presence burned through the terror, the way it felt to shed my old skin, even for a heartbeat, and go up in flames in his arms.

God, it was terrifying. The risk of it. The sheer, gnawing need.

But it was mine. Not fate's. Not his. This was mine to reach for. Mine to take.

My body moved before my mind could find a reason to stop. I curled my fingers around the thick muscles of his neck and tugged him down until our lips collided.

It started as a brush, featherlight, his mouth barely moving against mine. His heat rolled through me, not the scorching pain of memory, but a living warmth that grounded me, burning away the chill lodged deep in my bones. It was a careful dance, neither of us willing to be the first to devour the other.

But the hunger built, slow and tidal.

His hands came up to cradle my jaw, so carefully, as if my bones might turn to dust beneath his touch. My own hands splayed along his skull, memorizing ridges, the slickness of scale along the sharp arch of his cheekbones.

Every nerve ending in my body was awake, screaming for more as his mouth molded perfectly to mine.

The kiss turned greedy, gnawing at the ragged edges of something deeper, something wild and dangerous that lurked just beneath my skin.

Our first real kiss.

The one in the training grounds had ended with that panicked flight from everything I wanted and everything I feared. Now there was only this. Only the taste of his heat and the answering bite of my own need as our mouths slanted together, tongues tangling, the ghost of honey passing back and forth between us.

Omvar let out a guttural sound, half growl, half moan, and the vibration carved its way through every level of my being.

He scooped me up, his enormous arms pinning me to his chest. The stone of the doorframe dug into my shoulder blades. I wrapped my legs around his waist on instinct, locking us together at the hinge where desire and terror and hope met. My calves bracketed the iron bands of his hips, thighs trembling with the effort.

We pressed together, a mess of mouths and limbs. The only music was the sound of my ragged breaths. His body caged me in, but it wasn't the kind of cage I wanted to escape.

The solid wall of his chest was a barricade. His

hand cradled the back of my head, shielding me from the impact. I noticed with a savage sort of gratitude that his tail stayed away, curled safely behind him. He was giving me every inch of control. I knew, with a certainty that settled deep in my gut, that if I pushed him away, he would let me go.

Instead, my hips rocked into him, greedy and wild. The friction sent a jolt of pure fire through me, every clumsy grind stoking a bonfire at the base of my spine. I expected panic. Some part of me waited for terror to clamp down, for old memories to drag me under. But sensation flooded me, pure and bright and all-consuming. The solid feel of him pressed against me, the safety in the strength of his arms, the electricity of his mouth moving on mine.

For the first time in what felt like forever, I wasn't afraid. Omvar didn't trap me.

He sheltered me.

He pulled back, breath rough, his golden eyes blazing with a potent longing. His chest was a living furnace against my ribs, the mate-bond a hum between us. It was sharp, real.

This was my mate.

Holy. Crap.

His voice came out thick, words dragged from a

cracked, dangerous place. "We don't need to go any further." His tone quivered at the edges, a thread of control about to snap. "Only what you want."

The scramble of internal panic screamed for me to run, but it was drowned out by the ache low in my belly, and the way my skin buzzed under the weight of his gaze. I met his eyes, swallowing the fear one more time.

"I want this," I said. The voice was mine, but it sounded like someone else, someone reckless and utterly starved.

Relief hit his face, a wave, instantly bleeding into hunger. He crashed into me again, claiming my mouth in another bruising kiss, a wordless surrender to the gravity between us. My hands found his shoulders as he lifted me, carrying me as if I weighed nothing toward the sleeping platform that dwarfed my body.

He set me down with impossible care, every movement a negotiation between his raw strength and my human fragility. The platform's surface was warm, and I felt grounded, pinned to a new axis of pure sensation. His hands, callused and lethal, skimmed my sides. They never threatened, always waited for an order.

Omvar knelt beside the platform, muscles coiled

so tight he looked like he was fighting an urge to tear himself apart.

"I want to see all of you." The words slipped out, surprising me with their sudden need. But it was the truth. I wanted to see every inch.

Omvar straightened, chest swelling. For a moment, he just stared at me, pride and a bashful hope flickering in his gaze. Then he reached for the knot at his waist. I watched, helplessly mesmerized, as he stripped: first the battered wrap, then the tunic, peeling it away to reveal a body forged by violence and survival, both alien and beautiful. Every scar was a path leading to the core of him.

And then he laid a hand on the waistband of his trousers, his eyes fixed on me, asking for permission.

I nodded, sharp and helpless, my pulse frantic against my ribs.

He bared himself without hesitation.

His cock was alien and obscene and utterly hypnotic. Red scales glinted at the base in the yellow light of the room, fading to crimson flesh streaked with thick, black veins. At the tip, a mobile, fleshy lip flexed, twitching as if tasting the air—or waiting to taste me.

A bead of fluid gleamed at the opening, slick with anticipation. Beneath the strange sheath was a heavy weight that made my throat tighten, awe and disbelief warring inside me.

I'd felt it, fumbled with it in the dark, but seeing it in the open, seeing every impossible detail, was a challenge. This was not human. This wasn't even pretending.

I didn't hate it. Not even close.

My skin flushed with a want I couldn't name. Heat pooled between my thighs, a hunger that tore through the fear. I pressed my knees together and shivered.

Omvar's gaze went molten. The head of his cock dipped when he saw my reaction, the fleshy lip curling ever so slightly, as if begging for my attention.

"Touch yourself," I ordered, stunned again by the sound of my own voice.

A look of pleased surprise twisted Omvar's face. His hand wrapped around the thick, scaled base. He stroked, slow at first, then harder, the mobile tip rippling and flexing with each pass of his thumb. The alien rhythm of it was brutal and graceful all at once.

I watched, rapt. Absolutely fascinated. My fear dissolved under the onslaught, replaced by a breath-less, needy, aching want. I wanted to taste him, to ride him, to claim him in a language older than names.

He caught my eyes, holding me in the furnace of his longing. "Can I see you?"

Shyness warred with the fierce ache in my chest. I swallowed, my pulse thudding a heavy beat, and reached for the hem of my shirt. My hands trembled, but his gaze never left my body, tracking every inch of pale flesh as I bared it to the strange, hungry air of Scalvaris. When my shirt was gone, Omvar made a sound. It was low and wrecked, the kind of sound that made me feel powerful.

Admired. Wanted.

It made me bold. I shimmied out of my pants and bared myself completely, letting him see every scar, every imperfection. Every mark that had made me who I was. His pupils flared, bright and sharp. He hummed a note of desperate approval, his claws scraping softly against his own thigh.

Something wild possessed me.

I crooked a finger, beckoning him closer like some vixen from ancient media, the kind who took what she wanted and never looked back.

He surged across the platform, heat rolling off his skin to cover me in a protective, intoxicating shadow. His body bracketed mine, claws carving furrows into the blanket beside my thigh, but never touching me. The restraint in him was a jaw-clenching, painful thing to witness. I could see it in the flex of his biceps, in the tense coil of his wings.

We kissed, mouths crushed together, gasping in a frantic prayer. His tongue explored the seam of my mouth, the sharp spark of his taste, a blend of honey and fire, passing back and forth between us.

His claws, deadly and strong, curled under my thigh. He used the flat of them to nudge my knees apart, careful and gentle, never once scratching. His wings flared behind him, creating a cocoon of heat and shadow. My legs fell open, wide and welcoming, my nerves thrumming with the fear of being this exposed, and the wild power in letting him see me wrecked for him.

He didn't hesitate. Omvar dropped lower, his breath hot and unsteady on my thigh as he trailed open-mouthed kisses from my knee to my hip. His thick tongue, longer than any human's, started at my inner knee and made its way up, slow, torturous, leaving a slick, blazing line in its wake.

When he reached my core, I nearly jerked away, the shock of pleasure so sharp it hurt. His mouth sealed over my clit, his tongue flicking and swirling in a rhythm that stole every rational thought.

I collapsed backward, my spine arching, my fists gripping the twisted bedding above my head.

He was relentless. His tongue plunged inside me, then out, alternating between slow, worshipful swipes and rapid-fire flicks that sent shudders crashing through me. The tip was impossibly agile, pressing patterns into the swollen, needy flesh. His teeth grazed so gently that even the threat of pain amplified the pleasure.

His claws stayed splayed, carefully bracketing my thighs and hips, their lethal points catching the light but never once threatening. They curled just away from my skin, broadcasting the truth.

He could destroy me, but he was trying so hard not to. I'd never felt safer. I'd never felt more adored.

I let myself go. I let myself be devoured, cherished, undone by the firestorm building between my legs. The old terror was still there, an echo of cages and chains, but it was smaller than this. It was smaller than the want flooding my veins, smaller than the wild sound tearing from my throat, smaller than the way my body clenched and shook as Omvar coaxed every ounce of pleasure from me.

I came, loud and brilliant, pleasure shattering through me in shockwaves. I let myself scream, let the whole city know I was alive. Let them know I had survived. That I was his.

Not Skorai's, not Ignarath's, not a victim, not anymore.

When my body finally stopped twitching, I opened my eyes to find Omvar crawling up the length of me. His body moved like a predatory god, nothing human in his grace or hunger. He captured my mouth, kissing me deep. I tasted myself on his tongue, sweet and salty and new.

I wanted more. I reached for him, drawing him down until his weight bracketed mine, careful but unyielding. "Touch me there." My hand guided his, dragging his claws to my breast, to the aching heat between my thighs.

He followed every order. He kissed where I begged, his tongue rolling over every desperate inch. He asked for nothing and gave me everything.

The burning, unique pressure of his cock pressed against my entrance. The tip pulsed, weeping slick fluid, his scent wild and primal. "Are you ready?" His voice was hoarse, a guttural rasp.

"Yes," I gasped. "Now. Please."

He pressed in slowly, careful as ever, the ridged flesh stretching me with a heat and fullness unlike anything I'd ever known. The mobile lip worked against me, caressing my clit before he sank deep. The veins and scales provided a friction that rocketed me back toward the brink. Every pump drove him deeper, the heat and difference of him making my body ring like a struck bell.

We moved together, bodies slick and frantic, breath mingling. My hands grasped the sharp lines of his hips, pulling him into me, guiding his thrusts. He grunted, a raw, open sound, twisting his hips to grind that strange, writhing tip against every sensitive spot inside me. I sobbed his name, chanted it, my voice breaking each time lightning forked through my center.

I felt something ignite within me. It scorched every cell, burning away old scars and shame, leaving only the bright, impossible joy of being exactly where I belonged.

We came together, loud and undone, each of us clinging to the other in the wreckage of our own surrender.

Omvar's body shook, his roar muffled against my neck, his cock flexing inside me, releasing more heat and scent. I held him, held us, and let myself believe, for once, that healing could be this wild.

That it could be this real.

He collapsed beside me, gathering me under his

wing, our chests heaving together. Warm, dense silence spread between us.

I curled into him, a little raw, a little wild. My legs still quivered, every muscle slack with after-shocks. The stone was cool under my back. His body radiated heat, his scales sticky with sweat and pleasure.

He was stiff beside me, not quite at ease. His arm was locked tight, his gold eyes watching the door.

"No one will lay a claw on you as long as I breathe," he whispered, his voice a promise forged between worlds.

If I could believe in anything, I could believe in that.

OMVAR

MY MATE WAS MADE of a fire few could see.

Her newfound strength was a dangerous, beautiful thing. To cage her now would be to smother that flame, and I would rather be burned alive. I would gladly spend days with her in our rooms, making love until we remembered nothing else. But two days of mating frenzy was already more than we deserved with the threat of Ignarath still hanging heavy over us.

She needed a weapon.

Not just a wooden stick for drills, not the bundle of brittle human courage Scalvaris called training. I watched her cross the cavern's dust with a look on her face that was almost calm.

Only almost. She hid the exhaustion that

painted bruises under her eyes, burying it behind that stubborn set of her jaw. A survivor, yes. It was written in her knuckles and the way she never quite unclenched her fists.

But surviving wasn't enough. Not now. Not with Skorai's killers tasting the city air, hunting at the edges of Scalvaris territory. And the city could not protect her, not forever. I was done caging her. She needed a blade built into her bones. My lessons, not theirs.

I pulled in a slow breath. Scorched iron, old sweat, and sulfur pressed tight in the heavy stone air. "Take your position."

She flinched before she got control. The practice staff twitched in her hands—small, battered, the wood bearing a smear of her dried blood at one end. She gripped it like a lifeline, not a weapon. I saw it in her eyes, the old panic fighting to the surface, spine ramrod straight. Her mouth thinned in distrust.

"We don't have to do this," she said, her voice so tight it might snap. She met my gaze, chin stubborn, feet planted as if rooting herself in the sand to hold out forever.

I kept my bearing neutral, not yielding an inch of the space. My shadow, immense and molten with heat, fell over the lines she drew in her mind.

"What you know is not enough," I said. My voice came out a low rumble, the kind used to command soldiers in Ignarath pits. "Not against Ignarath. Not against what's coming. This is not a duel. You will forget your pride, or you'll die."

A flicker of something shone through, not quite anger, not quite fear. She squared her shoulders. "You saying you won't give me a choice?"

"They won't," I said.

She looked away, the silence thickening between us. Grit scraped the soles of her boots. I waited for her to run. Instead, she squared her shoulders, raised the staff until her pale knuckles stood out stark against the wood. "Fine."

Pride. Anger. Fear. All of it fuel.

I felt it coil in my chest like a living thing.

Now I meant to forge her into something that could not break. Even if it meant shattering the last clean pieces she had left.

I took a staff longer than hers, heavier, scuffed from decades of use by Drakarn muscle. My claws creaked along its length.

"Attack me. As you would anyone who means to kill you. Hold nothing back."

She charged without a second's hesitation, a flicker of desperate speed that would have tricked a fool. Not me. I let her come, didn't even move to block the first wild swing. The staff clipped my hip with a hollow slap that barely stung. Her breath was ragged, rhythm breaking already.

"Again," I barked.

She circled, staff held up, sweat darkening her brow. I saw her scan for an opening that a smaller opponent could exploit. She jabbed at my thigh, then my ribs. Fast, faster than I expected from someone who shook every morning, who woke with her mouth choked full of screams. Anger powered her, and the staff moved like an extension of her own need.

But not enough. She still held back.

"No," I snapped, catching her staff and wrenching it aside. Too gentle. "You're trying to win a sparring match. You should be trying to end a life. Stop thinking." I jerked her weapon further, spinning her off balance. She stumbled, heels scraping in the sand, and righted herself with pure, ugly determination.

Her jaw was tight. "I thought you were supposed to be teaching me."

"I am," I said. "Lesson one: there's no honor on

the dirt of Ignarath. If your enemy stumbles, you end them. You don't let them stand."

I didn't let her catch her breath. I lashed out, a controlled blow with the butt of my staff that she blocked, barely, the shock traveling up her arms.

"Don't stand tall. Your center of gravity is too high. Bend your knees!" I struck again, this one feinted at her shoulder, then slipping low for her thigh. She blocked, but the staff slid in her sweaty grip, and she barely kept it from dropping.

The air in the cavern thickened, echoing with the steady clack of wood and the grunt of effort. Heat crystals flickered above, throwing monstrous shadows against the black volcanic walls. Every misstep bounced around us, louder than a battle cry.

"Again!" I barked, because letting her rest was no mercy. The sound of her harsh breathing, the grit of sand under our boots, the sting of old fear sharp in her scent, every detail hammered into my brain, a map of her limits, her will.

She spat sweat from her lips, glared, and charged again. This time, I let her connect. The blow caught my forearm, a jolt of pain more satisfying than any easy win. I let the force knock my guard aside. In battle, holding ground gets you nothing. Surviving means yielding, striking back at the right moment.

"Good," I grunted. "Use your weight. Use surprise. This is not about trading blows until someone falls. It's about ending it before you bleed."

And then, when she staggered, breath hitching, hands shaking, eyes gone glassy with fatigue and shame, I pressed the lesson home.

"The most dangerous moment is when you're pinned," I said, circling her. "When your attacker is sure he has you and you think you're already dead."

She paled, the memory of every time she'd been held down flickering across her face, but nodded once. Absolute, fatalistic.

I moved in. Slowly, telegraphing every bared inch of threat. I didn't reach for her like a monster. I let her see me, let her brace, let her decide not to run. Then I swept low, my weight brute and unstoppable—her staff went one way, her body another. In a heartbeat, I caged her on the sand, one forearm pinning her shoulders, my chest pressing down. Just a technique, one that had saved my life a dozen times in Ignarath's pits.

But the stink of old fear erupted in my senses. I smelled it before she even moved. Pure, animal terror, hot, sharp, chemical. Her whole body went rigid beneath me, her eyes wide and lost, not looking at me but at something far away and terrible. I heard her breath snag, high and broken. Not resistance. Not anger. Just pure panic.

My own reflex screamed to finish the maneuver, to hold her down, force the lesson, make her fight through it. That was how Ignarath taught. Pain. Shame. You learned or died.

But I was not Ignarath.

Not anymore.

I released her. Slowly. Every movement open, hands showing, my body melting back off her before she even had to breathe. I pulled away, sat back on my heels, and forced my voice into something soft as sand after rain. "Deep breaths, *thravena*. Center yourself."

She blinked, a broken bird floundering back to the world, eyes darting across stone and shadow and finding me, still above her, but not a threat. Never a threat to her.

The tremors in her limbs broke to shame, then fury, then brittle exhaustion. She glared at me, burning with a pride that I would not break by force.

I sat and let her come back to herself. The

silence rang, full of everything I did not say. "That's right," I said. "We're not in Ignarath. It's me," I managed, aware of my claws digging so hard into my palms that I smelled blood. "You survived. That is more than most can say."

Her chest heaved, a wild flutter of breath. Her jaw worked, grinding back everything she wanted to say.

Then, raw and ragged, she shoved herself to her feet, bravado a shield of filth and fire. "Again," she rasped.

The demand was a gift.

I nodded once. If she wanted, I would give her the world all over again.

I pinned her. Not gentle, not slow, just enough to force the terror back, to make the lesson real. She didn't freeze. She snarled. The fear in her scent sharpened, laced with rage.

She exploded beneath me. Hips twisted, elbow slamming into my side in a move I'd shown her earlier. Pain cut through nerve and bone, a precise shot to an old wound. I grunted, shock scattering my thoughts, and she was out and gone, scrambling clear, staff up again.

A survivor forged in fire. Mine.

She stood over me, panting, forehead shining

with sweat, her body trembling from effort and adrenaline. Her eyes didn't hold terror. They burned with the victory of someone who had clawed their way out of hell and wanted witnesses to the scars.

I bared my teeth, a twisted smile. "Good."

The wariness never left her body, but her chin lifted. She had tasted power, and it was more intoxicating than any honey or gift. For a moment, we stood, two feral beasts, neither willing to break that new, tenuous peace.

I moved to the wall and slid down, passing her the battered waterskin. She took it, hand bumping against my claw in a flash of accidental intimacy. Her breath rasped, still hot with fighting, but the panic was gone. In its place lingered something sharper—resolve.

We passed the waterskin in silence, shoulder to shoulder. I noticed a fresh scrape along her arm, a thin line beaded with blood. I tensed, fighting the urge to snarl at myself. Blood always found her, even by accident.

She caught me looking, her mouth twisting as if she expected a lecture.

Instead, I nudged her arm. "Let me." I drew a clean cloth from my pack, something I always carried, a habit from years of patching up allies and rivals in the pits. She let me tend the wound, my big hands awkward around her delicate skin, but I kept the touch careful, reverent. I wiped away the grit, pressed the cloth to stop the bleeding, wrapped the cut with a strip torn from my shirt. Her pulse beat against my fingers, rapid but steady.

She leaned in closer. That small surrender flickered through me like hope, brittle and wild.

"Has there been any more news about those assholes from Ignarath?" Her voice was a ghost of the fire she'd shown moments before.

The frustration was a bitter taste in my mouth. "Nothing. The ones we captured remain stubbornly silent. The Council debates their next move, but they will not act." And every day they waited, the humans back in Ignarath suffered more.

Maybe they remained so impotent because they hadn't seen it.

Maybe they just didn't care.

Anger threatened to surge until my mate put her hand on top of my own and squeezed. It settled something wild deep within me.

"Come on, let's clean up our mess."

I began gathering the weapons. I hated the

waiting. Hated the not knowing. It felt too much like my time in Ignarath, watching and helpless.

A cold prickle skittered across the back of my neck. Old instincts flaring.

We weren't alone.

I straightened, weapon gripped hard enough to crack the haft. My eyes scoured the far wall, found nothing but pools of shadow where the light didn't reach. But I knew that feel, the way prey felt in the moments before a fight. The way I'd learned, from too many years of being the last beast standing, that you are never truly safe.

I stared into the dark until the silence hurt. Someone watched. Someone hunted.

But there was nothing there.

I stared for several long moments, but nothing moved except dust motes in the air. I gave the darkness a final glare.

If the shadows wanted a monster, they'd find one waiting.

This fight wasn't over.

Not by a long stretch.

I FORGOT pain could feel good.

My muscles screamed victory after the training session with Omvar. Every step was a triumphant agony. And the triumph lasted until we got to a small staircase and a whimper escaped me.

Yeah, this pain only felt good in theory. In practice, it still sucked.

For a moment, I tried to power through, but the burn in my thighs turned molten, and when my foot hit the first upward step, I lost the battle. The sound that escaped was a half-whined gasp, barely human, and nowhere near the kind of badass I'd hoped to be after taking on a Drakarn champion for an hour without dying.

Omvar stilled at my groan. He'd been off ever

since we left the caverns, looking over his shoulder like he expected a ghost to jump out of the shadows.

"Is everything all right?"

He jerked his head toward me, eyes tracking every breath I took, movements just a little too watchful. The question might as well have been chiseled out of stone. There was a brittle edge to it, tension vibrating through his bulk, as if he were walking into an ambush he half expected.

He answered himself before I could open my mouth. "It's fine."

Funny how "it's fine" in that tone of voice meant exactly the same thing as it did back on Earth, even though we were hundreds, if not thousands, of light-years away.

I forced a smirk, jaw clenched because any bigger movement made my neck spasm.

"You're in pain," he said.

"Letting a gigantic Drakarn throw me around for an hour will do that." There was a spark in the words, a flicker of humor and just a bit of pride even though my body had become a graveyard of aches, each bruise a souvenir.

I looked up at him, studying the way his jaw ticked, the way his wings hunched tighter. He wasn't just watching me, he was tracking every-thing: shadows, echoes, the unseen violence always lurking one stone corridor away. His scales caught the heat crystal's light, reflecting gold and blood-red, dangerous and battered, every line of him honed to the edge.

He reached over, slow enough for me to see the intent in every movement, and touched my arm. The contact sent a thread of fire down my nerves, his claws trailing lightly over my skin, delicate, measured.

The scrape wasn't pain, but the prick of purpose: not restraint, not a threat. Each claw tip barely skimmed my flesh until goosebumps erupted across my bicep.

He stopped, as if giving me every chance to pull away. I didn't. My body had learned to brace for pain, but his touch was a different kind of shock.

"I know what you need," he said.

I should have found that ominous. Instead, I felt the knot in my gut loosen a little.

He cocked his head, a silent order to follow, and turned into a side passage I hadn't noticed before: a narrow arch nearly hidden behind a spill of mineral-veined rock. The city's noise dulled as we slipped through, the world shrinking to the echo of our steps bouncing off slick, curving walls. I realized, with a flutter that was equal parts thrill and fear, that I'd never walked this path with anyone before. The air thickened, humid and strangely perfumed, carrying not just the scent of Drakarn but metallic steam and something almost sweet.

Omvar's steps were confident, predator's steps, calibrated for silence and dominance. Every so often, he glanced over his shoulder, reading my face, my every flinch, as if he needed proof I was still with him.

The tunnel opened abruptly, into light.

At first, I couldn't see. Steam rolled over the threshold, thick and curling in sheets off a pool so wide I couldn't find the far side through the haze. The scent hit me: minerals, copper, a sharp tang that stung my nose and made me think of old blood, but laced with something cleaner, restorative. The water was alive, its surface fractured by heat and shadow, reflections rippling across the glossy, volcanic stone.

Crystals embedded in the walls pulsed with a constant, mellow radiance, bright without glare. The light bent through the steam, painting everything in honey and bronze. No lamps, no harsh white light, just an endless warmth, as if the planet itself was holding its breath.

It felt like a secret world, carved by fire and time, meant for no one but us.

For once, I didn't crack a joke. Words felt too flimsy in the face of all that heat and shadow. I just stood there, heart hammering, aware I was trembling under Omvar's gaze.

I didn't have a swimsuit. Not that swimsuits were even a thing in Scalvaris.

The way Omvar was looking at me made me realize just how good that might be.

He watched me, not as a conqueror or a guardian, but as someone who wanted. The hunger in his eyes was raw, primal, but checked, a question, not a demand. My cheeks warmed, sudden and traitorous, but I didn't look away. Not now.

I slipped off my tunic and pants quickly, flinching against the muscle soreness and pretending I was braver than I felt. Every movement was an effort, pain zinging through my traps, my thighs. But I made it through, shoving away the old instinct to hide every inch of flesh.

I didn't cover myself. Not anymore. Not with Omvar.

I approached the pool, each step over slick stone

careful, my old armor falling away. Heat hugged my bare skin, the air so thick it clung to me, carrying the faint, metallic lick of minerals, the ghost of Omvar's scent tangled in the mist behind me.

The hot water was bliss.

The heat seeped into my skin and melted the tension from my bones. Every ache, every knot, every old ghost of pain burned away, replaced with an almost unbearable pleasure. I groaned, letting the sound escape for once, not caring how it might echo in the cavern.

I let my head fall back against the smooth rock ledge, my eyes drifting shut.

For four perfect seconds, I floated. The world shrank to the pulse at my neck, the way the water enveloped me, made my body feel weightless and possible again. The gentle slap of waves against my shoulders was the only sound, everything outside suspended.

The surface rippled as Omvar climbed in.

I almost opened my eyes, eager to see him, but the luxury of the heat was too much. I felt him settle behind me, the displacement of water, the pulse of something wild coming closer.

His hands, the ones that could crush stone, were impossibly gentle as they found my aching feet.

"Better?" he rumbled, his thumbs working circles into the knots of muscle there.

The touch sent a shiver up my spine. Not just from pleasure, but as a deep, animal memory flickered, warning me that hands could always become weapons. But Omvar's touch was measured, reverent, each pass of his thumbs learning my limits, listening to the tension in my body and working with it, not against it.

I didn't know he could be so gentle. I didn't feel even a hint of his claws.

"Mmm," was all I could manage.

The sound vibrated in my chest, a surrender and an invitation.

He chuckled, rough and low. "Not so tough now, are you?"

I snorted, forcing my eyes open enough to squint at him through the haze. His face was shadowed by the steam, scales gleaming in the golden glow, eyes half-lidded but sharp.

"Are you kidding? I bested you at least twice today."

Omvar's brows lifted. "I'm still standing, aren't I?"

I wiggled my toes in his grip, trying not to moan as he worked a particularly stubborn knot. "Only because you're the size of a cargo hauler. I barely dented you."

His thumb pressed a spot that made me see stars. "You dented me, *thravena*," he said, voice dropping a register. "I'll walk with the imprint tomorrow."

I bit my lip against a smile. It felt dangerous, letting pleasure and pride coexist, but I wanted to see how far I could push him. "Maybe next time I'll aim higher."

He grinned, wide and toothy. "If you aim higher, I'll have to retaliate."

"Promises, promises." I couldn't believe how easy this teasing was, how natural. How my body, so often a battlefield, felt like something worth fighting for.

He let go of one foot and picked up the other, his claws tracing idle, delicious lines over my arch. The roughness of his skin contrasted with the water-softness, a scrape edging toward tickle, but never crossing the line.

"You humans bruise like fruit," he said. "How do you survive anything?"

I laughed, breathy, the sound echoing oddly in the steamy air. "Belligerence and coffee. Too bad this planet's only got the first."

He made a soft sound, halfway between a growl and a laugh. His hands slid higher, up my calves, fingers lingering at my knee. His eyes tracked the progress, watching my breath, my reaction.

The touches became less therapeutic and more exploratory, turning into tender caresses and then hungry, water-slicked kisses.

He moved closer, the heat of his body a wall behind me. I caught the scent of him and let the water support me as I leaned back, my shoulder resting against his chest—his scales smooth and just barely yielding.

The room felt even more private now, the steam pressing in like a blanket, hiding us from the world's sharp edges.

Banishing the last shred of doubt, I reached for him.

I felt bold. Powerful. I wanted to taste him, to claim this moment, this feeling, as my own. I pulled his head down, my mouth finding his in the steam.

"I need you, Omvar. All of you."

His mouth was fire, open and searching, his tongue tracing the seam of my lips before slipping inside. The taste of him was heat and honey, made my head spin. His hands framed my face, tilting me up, a reverence in every movement.

He seemed to hesitate for a beat. His muscle tensed under my palms, as if holding himself back. But then, giving me plenty of time to pull away, he started to let his tail crawl up my leg while we kissed again.

He moved it slowly at first, the powerful muscle gliding through the water to wrap around my calf. The scales were smooth, the pressure a strange weight. He used it to pull me closer, then to trace patterns along my spine, my hips, my inner thighs.

The sensation was alien and wrong and exactly what I needed.

My body arched into the contact, nerves shorting out from the inside. I'd spent so long fearing the power in a Drakarn's touch, the way a tail could pin or a claw could wound. But Omvar's tail was an extension of his care—possessive, yes, but worshipful, marking me not as prey, but as something treasured.

He pulled me gently onto his lap, the water rising to caress my stomach. I felt the tip of his tail flick and tease at the juncture of my thighs, testing, always waiting for a flinch, a command to stop.

I didn't give him one.

His lips trailed along my jaw, down my neck, nipping just hard enough to make me gasp. His hands found my hips under the water, anchoring me, grounding me in the present. When his tongue flicked the shell of my ear, I lost the last of my composure.

I ground down, pressure and heat combining, the whole world contracting to the points where we touched. His tail cupped my ass, fingers splaying along my stomach, drawing me back against the hard, inhuman lines of his body.

A spike of anxiety lanced through me, sudden and brutal, a memory, a warning, the old terror that pleasure would always lead to pain.

I flinched.

He froze instantly, tail going slack, hands loosening. His mouth hovered at my throat, breath ragged.

"Do you want me to stop?" he whispered, the words soaked in adoration and uncertainty.

I pulled in a shaky breath and forced myself to look at him. His eyes, gold and fathomless, held nothing but devotion. Not demand. Not threat.

I focused on that gaze, anchored by the present and the steady pulse of his heart beneath my hand.

"I'm okay," I murmured. "I want this. Just … slower."

He nodded, the motion tiny but absolute. He

shifted, moving with infinite care, his tail only returning to its slow, deliberate strokes once I pressed back into him.

The water swirled, heat building again. He let his tail tease the insides of my thighs, tracing patterns that had no name, drawing pleasure where there had once been only terror.

The tip danced higher, nudging at my slick folds, never entering, just tasting, coaxing.

He kissed me again, slower now, his mouth speaking the same reverence as his body. Each touch was a plea, a promise, an act of worship.

"You're safe," he whispered into my skin. "You're mine, *thravena*. Only ever mine to claim."

The word settled into me, a healing balm and an electric shock.

His tail pressed higher, dipping into my wetness, stroking me in counterpoint to his mouth. The sensation was so new, so shockingly right, that waves of heat rolled over me. I bucked, arching, caught between pleasure and the old, hungry ache for control.

He let me set the pace. My hands found his shoulders, nails digging into his scaled flesh, and I rocked against his tail, chased the building storm.

His other hand moved to my breast, teasing, squeezing, every touch tuned to my need.

The climax came slow, then all at once: a shockwave tearing through the hollow of my body, a sob breaking free as I shattered on him, his name dissolving on my tongue. He held me through it, tail locked tight, arms a wall and a sanctuary all at once.

I collapsed against his chest, breath coming in harsh, needy gulps. He stroked my back, his tail holding me close as the aftershocks faded. I could feel the thrum of his arousal, the weight of his cock pressed against my skin, begging for permission.

I wanted him, all of him.

I turned, rising above the fear, finding a new kind of boldness in my battered bones. I straddled his lap, water sheeting off my skin.

"More," I said, voice hoarse with want, with hope.

His eyes widened, a flash of helpless awe before I took him in hand. The feel of him, hot, ridged, the mobile lip at the head flexing under my grip, sent a bolt of power through me.

I guided him to my entrance, both of us slick with water and need. He watched my face, checking for the faintest tremor or recoil. I gave him none. I was in control, guiding him into me inch by inch, letting the strange, beautiful friction stretch and fill me.

He let out a guttural moan, hands bracing my hips, but didn't thrust, didn't force. I rocked, slow, learning his body and my own all over again.

The world narrowed to the place where we were joined, to the water sloshing around us, to the heat crystal's glow gilding our skin. I moved, claiming every inch, every thrust, chasing pleasure and erasing old ghosts.

"*Thravena*," he said the word over and over again, that special name that was only mine.

Another wave of pleasure built and built until it finally cascaded over me, taking Omvar with it. I felt completely safe, cherished, dissolving into him as he roared his release into my neck, his tail curling around my waist.

After, we lingered, entwined in the scented, mineral-rich pool, content, safe, sated.

I could live in the bath forever.

We were tangled together in the warm, quiet water, my head resting on his chest, his wings a half-submerged canopy around us. I'd never felt so peaceful, so whole. A soft, hopeful laugh bubbled up from my chest.

For one crystalline moment, I let myself believe in it.

A sharp, urgent voice shattered the quiet.

"Omvar!"

A Council runner stood silhouetted at the cavern entrance, his posture rigid with alarm. "The Blade Council requires your presence. Now."

THE HEAT OF HER SKIN, the scent of her release, the impossible peace of the afterglow. All of it evaporated in the cold, sharp summons from the Council. One moment, she was a warm, sated weight in my arms. The next, I was a warrior again, the city's problems crashing back.

The air shifted, thick with the tang of sulfur and the faint sweetness that still clung to our bodies. Her hand flinched where it rested against my chest, nails digging into a scale as she blinked awake, confusion turning to dread in her eyes.

The cocoon of the bath shattered.

The city was calling me back, demanding its beast. My muscles tensed. I was already arming myself in my mind.

"Go back to our quarters," I ordered, my voice harsher than I intended as I climbed from the water with her at my side. "Lock the door."

Reika's eyes widened, the blissful peace already replaced by a familiar, wary tension. She shrank into herself, knuckles whitening on the edge of her towel. For a heartbeat, she looked as if she might argue, insist on coming, but the predator in my voice cut her down.

I hated leaving her. Hated it more than I'd hated anything in my life.

I hated the beast I became when crisis called. Hated how fast my tenderness became the weapon everyone feared.

She nodded, silent and resigned, lips pressed in a thin line. The scent of her fear stung my senses, a bitter smoke on the air. My guilt was a hot, spiked thing, but there was no time for softness now.

I dressed quickly, yanking on the rough tunic, the collar chafing my throat where her lips had marked me. My body was still humming from her touch, the aftershocks of pleasure crawling raw beneath my skin. I forced my hands to steady, fighting to bury the urge to turn back, to gather her up and shield her from the world.

Scalvaris did not tolerate hesitation. Especially not from me.

I pulled on my belt and blades, the familiar weight a cold comfort over fresh wounds. The bath's steam clung to my skin as I strode into the tunnels, every sense tightening, head on a swivel, devouring every scent, every echo off the walls. I scanned the dark corners, the beaded glimmer of moisture on obsidian, the way the heat crystals flickered as if threatened by my passing. Gone was the honey-thick air of safety. The chill pressed in, turning sweat to ice against my spine. My nostrils flared, drawing in the city, damp, mineral, blood-metal, and threat.

Shadows deepened ahead, stone sweating in the chill shift of the city's pulse. My footsteps, deliberate and silent, echoed over slick floor. The afterglow had calcified into vigilance.

I found Nyx waiting for me outside the interrogation chambers. His scales gleamed under the pitiless light, the blue-black plates burnished with readiness. Arms crossed over his chest, he looked carved from midnight stone, eyes hard and sharp.

"They caught one trying to sneak in through a sky vent," he said without preamble. "Ignarath," he spat. "He won't talk. Says he'll only speak to the great traitor himself." His lips twisted. "Lucky you."

The Great Traitor.

I couldn't decide if that was better or worse than the Beast. The city's whispers had followed me all my life, but Ignarath's poison ran deeper than anything Scalvaris could conjure.

I gave Nyx a nod and jerked my chin toward the cell door. "Let's see what the bastard wants."

The chamber stank of power and pain. Ancient stone walls hunched over a floor slick with old blood. Heat crystals perched high above, their light harsh and twitching, casting every shadow sharper and deeper, as if the darkness itself was waiting for a chance to strike.

There was no comfort there, only the memory of violence, the taste of metal on the tongue. The air was thick with the scent of fear, sweat, and the acrid tinge of shackles left too long in the damp.

In the center, chained to an iron ring set deep in the floor, sat Dravka. Purple scales stretched taut over corded muscle, spiked and glistening where the lamplight struck. A cruel smirk twisted his wide mouth, revealing fangs stained with the remains of whatever he'd bitten through since capture. His wrists bled where the shackles cut, but he wore those wounds like old medals, every bit as defiant as when we'd first met in Ignarath.

His eyes, yellow and bright as venom, found me the instant I entered. My presence meant nothing to him. Not fear. Not respect. Just the old rivalry, the old contempt. Skorai's favorite snake-in-the-sand, the champion whose blades were always slick with poison, whose pleasure was found in others' agony. He rattled his chains in greeting.

"Omvar," Dravka sneered, the sound curling off his tongue like a challenge. "Playing hero for the weaklings of Scalvaris?"

Muscles bunched beneath my scales. I let the insult hang between us, let his confidence echo off the walls, feeding his arrogance. I knew his game.

The only way to win against Dravka was never to play by his rules.

"You wanted to talk. So talk." I kept my voice level, a cold, flat thing.

He grinned wider, rolling his shoulders, letting the chains rattle and ring. The noise was calculated, a performance for our benefit. He wanted to remind me of the bonds I'd once worn, of Ignarath's ability to cage even its best monsters. He was chained, but his posture was pure predator, leaning forward until the shackles bit, head canted as if listening for the sweet sound of a scream.

"Talk?" he drawled, savoring every syllable. "Why would I waste words on rabble? You've traded the scent of victory for the stink of desperation. Look at you. Scalvaris's lapdog. Broken, caged, sniffing after the humans like they're worth more than blood on the sand."

I didn't blink. Didn't waver.

Inside, the old rage simmered, warred with shame and the sticky residue of Reika's touch. I hated the taste of violence, but it lived inside me, coiled and waiting. Every word Dravka spat was meant to draw it out, to make me brutal, to prove I had never changed.

He rattled his chains, a savage music meant for my ears alone. "Did they let you keep your claws, Traitor? Or did you hand them over with your spine?"

I forced a flat smile, stepping closer so he could smell my conviction, not my fear. "You want to test me, Dravka? You can try. But you'll lose more than dignity."

He just laughed, low and rough, a sound like grinding stone. "You've been so busy playing guard dog for your little human pet ... so focused on the one cage." He leaned forward, his eyes gleaming with malicious triumph. "Did you even notice the other doors swinging open?"

Ice. Pure, arctic ice flooded my veins. He wasn't a threat.

He was a distraction.

The realization snapped through me with the sharpness of a fresh blade. The slow, showy infiltration. Letting himself be seen. Asking for me, of all people. His presence here was no accident. It was theater.

A decoy.

I took a step back. My mind raced, summoning every detail Nyx had given me, every security protocol I'd ever mapped through these tunnels.

Whatever was happening, it was already underway. The humans. The enclave.

Reika.

Panic ripped through me, primal and undeniable. The city wasn't holding its breath because it trusted me to solve this. It was waiting for the wound to open.

I was out of the cell in a heartbeat, my mind racing. "He's stalling," I snarled at Nyx. "He wanted to get caught. He's playing with us."

Nyx's eyes widened, every bit as ruthless as mine

in that instant, the warning sinking in. I grabbed him by the shoulder before he could move.

"Get to the human enclave," I roared. Protocol, politics, none of it mattered. "Check on all of the humans. Now!"

He didn't waste time with questions. Nyx sprinted away without a word, his footsteps pounding down the corridor, echoing like war drums. The world narrowed to action, to the pulse of duty and desperation crashing together.

I was torn. My every instinct screamed to run back to my rooms, back to Reika. But the other humans … they were vulnerable. Unprotected. I saw their faces in a flash: Kira, Selene, Eden, Kinsley, and more. My claws flexed, scraping deep gouges in the stone, anchoring me to the moment.

She wouldn't forgive me if I left them to suffer.

I broke into a run, my claws scrabbling for purchase on the stone, heading for the distant human quarters. My heart hammered against my ribs, each beat a prayer and a curse.

Stones flew beneath me. Air moved sharp and fast, the scent of blood rising ahead, Ignarath, thick and unmistakable, slicing through the rich stew of market and river and sweat. I tore through the tunnels, vision narrowing, body reduced to need and velocity. Reika's name rang behind my teeth, but I forced it back. Duty first. Hope later.

A new sound cut through the wail of the alarm, echoing from a side tunnel up ahead, followed by the unmistakable roar of Drakarn under attack.

I crashed forward. The city's veins boiled with panic and resistance. Up ahead, the darkness flickered with the strobe of enemy blades, the ring of Drakarn war cries, the shrieks of Ignarath's invaders punching into Scalvaris's heart. I heard steel on stone, felt the deep-throated bellow of a warrior cut down, the sick heat of another death thrown like a torch into the dark.

The world was burning, and I was already too late.

OUR QUARTERS.

I kept repeating the words in my head, as if I might transform their meaning into something less loaded, less dangerous. But there was no mistaking what Omvar had said. I could still hear the deep roll of his voice, echoing in my head.

Our quarters.

At first, I'd thought I'd misheard. Or maybe hallucinated. Maybe I was overtired or still riding the aftershocks of a nightmare. But that was definitely what Omvar had said.

Our quarters.

I sat there, the syllables clattering around. The possessiveness of it, the assumption, sent a prickle of alarm down my spine.

Was it logical after the whole mate declaration? Sure.

Did I give a damn?

Not even a little.

So I didn't go back there, despite his instructions.

My pride was a knife I gripped in my fist, pressing the edge to my palm until sense bled away. I wasn't property, certainly not his, not anyone's. I was nobody's "ours." Not after everything I'd bled for to claw my way out of cages.

I needed to see my own people, to remember who I was when a seven-foot-tall, red-scaled warrior wasn't taking up all the air in the room. The solid stone corridors held familiar, old shadows as I turned away from the path Omvar had expected—ordered—me to take. The farther I walked, the more my uncertainty melted into stubbornness, daring the city itself to disagree.

I wouldn't be claimed. I wouldn't be domesticated, no matter how soft the bedding or how steady his heat against my back.

Not that they had soft bedding in Scalvaris.

The human quarters smelled of stale sweat and scorched rock, a stew of bodies and humid air. My breathing eased as the shape of the tunnels changed, low ceilings crouching above the carved stone cells, footsteps echoing in the semi-dark. There, even sulfur was familiar, overpowering, yes, but it didn't scare me the way new things did.

My old room greeted me without ceremony. It felt smaller than I remembered, the stone sleeping platform barely a suggestion of comfort. I sat, hugging my knees to my chest, letting the rough blanket dig into my shins, the surface unyielding beneath my weight. The room was mute, lifeless.

It felt very small and not at all like mine.

My heart did a slow, bitter circuit, bouncing off the memory of Omvar's space, the low thrum of heat, the way his scent clung to every fabric until my skin prickled just walking through the threshold. Maybe Omvar's quarters really had become home.

How strange.

I tried to shake off the thought. I couldn't decide if it was more terrifying that I wanted that home, or that I'd started to believe I could belong there.

A sharp rap at the stone frame. "Reika? Omvar let you out of his sight?" Vega stuck her head in my doorway and offered me a lopsided grin.

Her hair was a wild, coppery halo, the only

thing bright in the half-light. Her voice, low and teasing, should have stung, but it didn't. I would have expected a bite with her question a few months ago. She'd been the one most suspicious, most defensive, of us all. But she'd found her own mate in Zarvash and now definitely understood the appeal of the Drakarn.

I shot her a half-hearted glare, the edge blunted by exhaustion and a flicker of relief. "He was called to the council. Any idea why?"

Vega rolled her eyes, stepping farther into the room and leaning against the wall. "Zarvash has been in the council chambers all day. More of this Ignarath bullshit."

The room felt less empty. She picked at a loose thread on her sleeve, her sharp gaze flicking to me and holding for a moment, weighing my tension, maybe sensing that I was ready to bolt at the slightest provocation. I wanted to ask her about home, about safety, about what it meant to rest with a Drakarn's arm flung over your waist in the dark and not want to run screaming. But that wasn't a conversation for that moment.

We talked about nothing in particular, her words brusque but steady. She brought up council rumors, the scrape of politics inside the chambers, whispering about the creepy new priest and the tension between the temple zealots and the warriors.

She was keeping me company, making me feel safe. Included. Like this place really might be where I belonged.

My pulse slowed, the air tasting marginally less toxic. Whatever this was, it sounded routine, council squabbling, Drakarn pride, not an omen of doom. Maybe I could let myself breathe, imagine the city might hold a day without bloodshed.

Then a noise cleaved the air.

Not the low scrape of worry, not the ordinary rattle of pipes or the distant ring of forges, but something sharper.

A scream. Terrified.

Human.

My body recoiled. Every instinct I had screamed at me to run, to find a hole and burrow deep. The old Reika would have.

She would have frozen like a deer in a hunter's sights.

But I wasn't her anymore. Not completely.

Omvar's training, the bruises still blooming on

my skin, the phantom ache in my muscles, it all kicked in. There is no honor on the dirt of Ignarath. The words were a brand, cauterizing panic into action.

I didn't run away.

I ran toward the sound with Vega right behind me.

Stone bit at my feet, the corridor's shadows flickering under frantic, broken light. My heart hammered, a thunder that drowned out everything else. I could hear my own breath, ragged, desperate, mixing with the trouble ahead.

The corridor was chaos.

A table stood overturned, two of the smaller human women, Kinsley and Eden, crouched behind it. They hurled anything they could grab: battered bowls, cracked mugs, a length of pipe. Each missile sailed through the air, only to be batted away by the two Drakarn standing before them, brown-scaled, brutish, massive.

The Drakarn moved with a bored, almost casual violence, their arms sweeping the air, fangs bared in hungry grins. The table shuddered with every blow, stone splintering under the onslaught.

"Shit," Vega hissed at my side. I caught the glint

of her blade, her posture shifting to fight, but I grabbed her arm—it was a reflex, an order, a plea: don't get killed, not today.

Then I saw him.

A third Drakarn stepped into the dim light, and my stomach dropped, bile surging up my throat. I stumbled, legs suddenly weak, a cold fire racing through me.

Draskeer.

His scales were the color of a fresh bruise, his face a mask of cruel, familiar arrogance. A guard from the Ignarath slave pens. A tormentor from my nightmares. The sight of him sent a spike of pure, cold terror through my heart.

I would never forget his laugh.

My breath caught. My limbs went numb. For one horrible, sinking moment, the world dissolved into the roar of the arena, the clang of chains.

No. Not again.

Omvar's voice was a low growl in my memory. Stop thinking. End it before you bleed.

Draskeer's eyes locked on mine, hungry and cunning, his smile a sharpened blade. "Little prey! I knew you couldn't hide forever."

I didn't answer. I charged, grabbing a fallen

training staff someone must have brought back from the training grounds.

My body moved before thought could root me to the spot. The staff was an extension of my hands, my rage, my old wounds.

I barreled forward, running into the fray, not with caution, but with everything I'd learned since the last time I was a victim. The air was thick with the reek of sweat, scorched dust, and the iron tang of my own fear.

The first Drakarn lunged for me, claws slicing through the air. I ducked, rolling beneath his outstretched arm. I swung the staff in a low arc. I remembered Omvar's voice, the lesson was pain and precision, not honor.

I was not just defending; I was attacking. I aimed for joints, for knees, for anywhere flesh was vulnerable beneath those impossible scales. The staff found a target: a knee. The sound was a meaty, satisfying thunk, followed by a roar of pain and surprise as the Drakarn buckled, clutching his leg. It wasn't a killing blow, but it was enough to prove that I was no longer the frozen prey he expected.

Vega was at my back, hurling a bowl straight into the eye of the second Drakarn, who staggered, then turned on her with a bellow. The table shielded Kinsley and Eden for another heartbeat, but it wouldn't last.

Draskeer prowled forward, his focus locked on me. "You're not hiding well enough this time, little prey," he crooned, his voice digging under my skin. "You belong on your knees."

My mind flickered, the memory of chains and sharp, metallic laughter trying to drag me down. But I wouldn't let it. Not now. Not for him.

Every muscle screamed as I lashed out again, the staff cracking against Draskeer's forearm, scraping scales until they bled.

He barely flinched. He grinned, the smile a promise and a threat.

Kinsley's scream rose again, a thin, terrified thread. One of the Drakarn seized her by the arm, wrenching her bodily over the barricade as she kicked and thrashed. Eden tried to help. She lunged, only to be disarmed and thrown to the ground, a massive foot pinning her.

Kira appeared at my elbow, wide-eyed, clutching a broken chair leg. When had she shown up?

"Do something!" she panted, but the words barely registered. The world was sound and motion, a mess of blows and snarls.

Vega fought with desperation, a wild animal hissing, driving her blade into the side of the Drakarn's thigh. He howled but didn't fall. Blood streaked the wall as he yanked her aside and flung her into the far wall. She slumped, dazed but alive.

I locked eyes with her across the chaos, my voice catching against the words I couldn't shout. My mouth formed the words: get help.

She hesitated, the need to fight burning in her eyes, but she nodded. She faded into shadow, sliding away as silent as breath.

I had seconds left.

Draskeer surged forward, batting my staff aside like a twig, his strength overwhelming. His claws wrapped around my arm, the grip a brand of iron I remembered all too well.

"You've learned some new tricks," he sneered, his breath hot and foul against my face. "It won't be enough."

He dragged me backward, my heels scraping uselessly against the stone.

A last glance over my shoulder—Eden cowered on the floor and met my gaze, eyes wide and wild, a storm of terror and grief. She was shaking with a hopelessness I knew intimately.

I wouldn't let her break. I wouldn't let myself break.

Stone bit at my back as Draskeer hauled me into a dark service tunnel. The world shrank to the scrape of claws, the copper stench of defeat, Eden's silent scream echoing behind me. But inside, something fierce held on—a refusal, a ragged promise.

Not this time. Never again.

THE CITY WAS A SCREAMING WOUND, and I was the blade defending it.

Drums hammered the air, sounding off slick, black stone. The rhythm was relentless, a battlefield heartbeat, a fever running beneath my scales. My own pulse fought to break free, kicked and battered at my ribs, so loud I could barely hear the world.

Down there, beneath all those tons of volcanic rock, shadows and sickly yellow light flickered and brawled against the walls, making the tunnels churn and shift in the corners of my eye.

Scalvaris was chaos.

Stone corridors flashed past, the world reduced to blurred motion, Nyx a silent streak of storm-dark scales on my right, Khorlar on my left, his jaw clenched, eyes narrowed into slits. The stench of air was thick: Ignarath filth, scorched metal, the sharp tang of spilled Drakarn blood.

How many? Where? How?

The questions spun, merciless as windblown grit. My mind latched onto them, a predator refusing to let go. This city was supposed to be guarded, its veins patrolled by blades, its entrances a promise that violence couldn't slip inside. So how had they gotten in? Who opened the wound?

Rage was a cleansing fire. It blazed through my veins, devouring caution, scouring away the endless calculations and regrets simmering in the back of my mind. I let it burn down the politics, the careful dance around status and suspicion, the ancient weight of blood debts and shame. There was only the hunt.

We moved as one, locked in step by shared purpose and the pure, ugly music of fury. We were a beast with three heads, tearing through the city's heart. Our claws dug channels in the stone, tails lashing, each stride fueled by memory and dread.

"We found two dead guards by the eastern sky shafts," Khorlar roared over the din. "That will take them near the human quarters."

I didn't need him to tell me. The scent was thick on the air, an acrid trail of blood, terror, and weaker prey. Human sweat was different—sweet, alien, coppery, rising above the tangle of Drakarn fear and the greasy stench of Ignarath. The path burned in my nose; I could almost see it, a red thread winding through the labyrinth.

We sprinted, every footstep a promise I could not afford to break.

The tunnel bent, and the world exploded into violence.

The human quarters were chaos incarnate. The stone floor was slick, a crust of half-dried blood, footprints glimmering beneath scattered globs of heat crystal wax. Two Drakarn guards lay crumpled near the threshold, their scales shredded, throats vented to the bone.

The walls were battered, flecked with handprints and the desperate arcs of fingers dragged during the last moments of a struggle. I tasted iron on the air, thick and choking.

Screams slashed the silence. Human, Drakarn —there was no difference when the pain was deep enough. The noise rebounded, multiplied by the low ceiling, the roundness of the alcoves.

The Ignarath infiltrators came in tight formation, a hand-picked squad wielding their discipline like a chain. Not a pack of wild brutes, not a roving mob. Each movement was calculated, lines of attack closing with the cold, surgical precision only years of blood games could breed. They pressed forward, step by step, no wasted motion, no unnecessary sound.

I let the Beast of Ignarath off its leash.

My claws were for tearing.

My fangs were for rending.

There was no room for gentleness there. The old, black part of me, the one carved by Skorai's hand, reveled in the violence.

This was what I was made for. To be the monster that hunted other monsters.

I moved through the enemy ranks like a scythe, every blow a killing strike. Bone snapped under my fists. My claws found throats, the hot gush of arterial blood painting the stones. The Ignarath fought hard but not like me.

No one fought like me.

I slammed one to the ground, felt the ridge of his spine yield, crushed it beneath my knee. Another, smaller, tried to flank me; I twisted, caught his blade, snapped his wrist, finished him with a single, silent bite to the throat.

There was beauty in it, the rhythm of destruction, a dance I'd been bred for, a language older than words. I heard Nyx's battle cry and saw Khorlar sweep his tail to knock two enemies from their feet. We moved with the storm, unafraid of the blood, unafraid of ourselves.

This wasn't random. This wasn't chaos. It was a slaughter. Assassins. Their faces were stripped of joy or fear. Only focus, and the drive to kill or die.

A scream cut the air. I spun—

Kinsley, one of the humans with courage enough to start a riot in her sleep, was being dragged away, kicking, spitting curses. Her captor was massive, scales scored by the scars of a hundred pit fights. I bellowed a challenge, a sound that would have broken a lesser Drakarn, but another Ignarath intercepted, blade flashing at my throat.

Khorlar and Nyx broke off, their priorities shifting as humans scattered, vulnerable. Nyx pulled Kira, stunned, pale, blood splashed across her face, from the clutches of a dying Ignarath.

Khorlar scooped up Eden, her arm limp and hanging, blood streaking her sleeve. The squad's formation threatened to collapse, but they redoubled, fighting not for glory, but for their deadly mission.

A shadow flickered in the corner of the melee.

"Where did these bastards come from?" Vega seemed to materialize out of nowhere, a wickedly sharp knife clutched in her hand, blood streaked up to her wrist. Her eyes were wild, hair plastered to her temples. "Three attacked us. And now this?"

I was a breath away from responding, some growled reassurance rising in my throat, when I saw him.

Draskeer.

The same guard I'd done my best to keep away from Reika in Ignarath. Skorai's pet bruiser, a specialist in pain. The bruise-scaled bastard.

My vision tunneled. Draskeer's arm was a band of iron around Reika's waist, his claws digging into her as he dragged her, writhing, into the shadows at the far end of the corridor. The panic in her eyes was a knife under my ribs.

My world snapped, crushed by the mate-bond. The fury that tore out of my chest had nothing to do with honor or Scalvaris or even vengeance.

A sound of pure, world-ending fury rose in me —no longer a warrior, but a mate being robbed.

"Omvar! Secure the others!" Khorlar's voice was a distant irrelevance, his order drifting like wind-blown ash.

The bond screamed. A singular, burning command that superseded rank, strategy, and reason.

Find her.

Save her.

It drowned out everything else. I saw only the space where she had been, the bruises on Draskeer's arms, the glint of his fangs too close to her skin. I couldn't hear the battle behind me. I couldn't hear Nyx's shout or Khorlar's curses.

There was only the bond. Only the hunt.

I disengaged from the warrior in front of me with a brutal, final blow that sent him staggering back, his chest caved in. The wet crack of bone was an afterthought. I didn't wait for him to fall, ignoring the sprays of blood clinging to my arms. I left the others to the chaos; all that mattered was the fading scent of her fear, sharp as raw copper, and the foul stench of Draskeer's trail, like rotten eggs and poison musk.

My mind was a maelstrom: guilt, terror, longing, the twin engines of shame and desperation twisting every nerve raw. I had promised her safety. I had promised myself I would stand between her and all the monsters of this world. And now she was gone, snatched into the dark by the worst Ignarath had ever bred.

I launched myself into the darkness after them.

The stone passage narrowed, rough-hewn walls scraping my wings, the air cooler, thick with the echo of my footfalls and the distant, rhythmic thump of the city's alarms. Every sense stretched to breaking. I could smell them, the acidic reek of Draskeer, carrying the old ghosts of the arena, and beneath it, the fragile sweetness of Reika's skin, her terror a trail I could track even blind.

My side burned.

I realized, distantly, that I was hurt, a deep gash in my ribs, blood seeping hot and sticky down my flank. I didn't feel it. I didn't care.

There was only the trail, slick and cold and metallic, winding through unmapped stone, through secret ways I hadn't known existed. These were the old tunnels, forgotten even by the city's lifeblood. They spiraled and twisted, black as the world before creation.

I stumbled, righted myself, shoved forward, reckless as the beast I was raised to be.

In these tunnels, every shadow was an enemy. My feet slipped on blood, stone slick beneath my claws. My heartbeat thundered, a savage drum drowning out even the alarms. I barely saw the walls, the smears of old battle, the broken doors kicked in by desperate hands.

I drove myself forward, chasing the ghosts and the scent and the memory of what I would never forgive myself for—too slow, too weak, too late. Guilt and terror blurred together until I was nothing but a predator chasing the last warmth of hope.

The tunnel opened up into the searing glare of the volcanic wastes. The wind howled, ripping at the lingering traces of scent—Draskeer, Reika, blood and panic—almost lost, but not quite. The world outside was a red desert, shimmering with toxic heat, stone whipped into knives by the gale. The ground was a mosaic of cracked obsidian and glass, the sky a boiling cauldron of twin suns leering down.

The trail was faint there, the wind tearing at the scent, but it was enough.

I didn't hesitate.

Bloodied, battered, and alone, I vanished into the shimmering red desert.

I was the blade. The city was a wound. If I failed, if I hesitated, everything would bleed out.

But I was not what Ignarath made me. I was

something else. I was the monster they should have feared all along.

And I would burn the world to bring her home.

22

REIKA

THE AIR WAS a punch to the face. Hot. Sharp. Thick with the smell of sulfur and baked rock. Draskeer's grip was an iron cage on my bicep, claws digging deep as he dragged me into the volcanic wilds, a hellscape of shattered stone under a sky that bled. Every jarring step was a reminder. I was a prisoner again.

There was nowhere to run. Nowhere to hide.

Every sense screamed danger. The volcanic crust cracked under my boots with each uneven step. Heat pressed down, a physical weight that turned each breath into a punishment. When the wind shifted, it drove the chemical bite of minerals down my throat. It was the kind of air that scorched you from the inside out, a fire in the lungs, burning hotter with every gasp.

With each step, Draskeer yanked me forward, his claws digging deeper. I couldn't stop seeing old blood pooled in the cracks of the stone, real or just a phantom of memory.

I didn't dare stagger or let him see the tremor that shook my muscles beneath a stubborn posture. He had known all my tells once, but I wasn't the same girl he'd tormented in the pens.

And yet, my body tried so hard to betray me. My skin prickled where his claws pressed, a phantom ache of memory. Still, my mind scrambled for a weapon—for Omvar's voice hissing through the cracks.

You are not prey. Not anymore.

"You're quiet, little prey," Draskeer sneered, his voice scraping against my nerves. "Remember how you used to cry? I miss that sound."

He wanted me whimpering. Wanted me to collapse under the weight of old terror. My mouth went dry. My heart stuttered, a frantic bird desperate to beat out of my chest. The stink of him, hot stone and copper and something spoiled, was an overwhelming wave. I stumbled but caught my balance, planting my feet on the grit.

Omvar's voice echoed in my head. *Your center of gravity is too high.*

I sank into a lower, more stable stance, my body remembering lessons my screaming mind had almost forgotten. I closed my eyes for half a heartbeat, letting the memory of Omvar's coiled strength bleed into my bones. Not prey. Not prey. Exhale. I bent my knees, spreading my feet over the sharp red sand. The urge to run pounded at the base of my skull, a frantic, useless drumbeat.

The sound of my blood was thrumming a war drum in my ears.

I opened my eyes.

"I remember you being a coward who hides behind bigger monsters," I spat back, the words a victory on my tongue. "Is Skorai not here to hold your hand today?"

I forced myself to look him in the eye, to meet his gaze with all the venom I could muster. The words tore like claws in my throat, but I savored them. Insults were armor. If I kept my mouth moving, he wouldn't hear the sobs rattling behind my teeth.

His grip tightened, fury flashing in his eyes. "You've grown a tongue. I'll cut it out before I take you back."

That threat should have made me shrink. It almost did. My jaw clenched so hard I felt my teeth grind. The memory of torn skin, of screaming while no one came, flashed hot and sharp beneath the surface. But I forced myself to stay tall, to meet his rage with the only weapon I had left: defiance.

He shoved me toward a jagged spire of rock. My abused hands scraped against the rough surface as I broke my fall. Pain lanced up my arms, sharp and insistent. I hissed between my teeth, biting back the whimper he craved. My knees stung where I'd landed on the heat-scoured stone, grit already grinding into the fresh cuts.

But I didn't linger on the pain. My instincts howled for an escape. A weapon. Anything. I pressed my cheek to the rock, my eyes roving the ground. A slice of obsidian. A crack just wide enough for a desperate hand. Not much, but maybe enough to draw blood.

I dragged myself upright before he could decide to help me, my jaw set. My breath came in ragged spurts, every inhale burning. Draskeer loomed above me, his tail cutting slow, satisfied arcs through the air. He wanted to see me break. Wanted proof that the weak little human was still in there, begging.

Not this time.

I spat blood from a split lip, the iron taste sparking somewhere old and bitter. "Is this it?" I sneered, fighting to keep the tremor from my voice. "You had to drag me out here just to feel like you have any power left at all?" My breath hitched, but I pressed on. "Was Skorai too busy licking his wounds after Zarvash stole his champion? Or did he just send you because he knows you're the only one desperate enough to go?"

His tail snapped against the ground, spraying grit across my ankles. He bared his fangs. "You'll wish you'd remembered how to beg, prey."

I saw the spasm of anger, the flicker of hesitation in his glare. Good. I wanted him mad. I wanted him sloppy. Omvar's lessons ran through my mind, clear and cold. An enemy who loses control gives you an opening. Survive the first, bestial rush. Let him bleed out his temper.

I would choke on my own tongue before I gave him the satisfaction of my fear.

He laughed, a grating, ugly sound. "Your Beast can't save you out here." He raised a cruel-looking blade, its serrated edge gleaming in the harsh light. He was drawing this out, savoring my terror like a fine meal.

My mouth went dry. I tasted old horror on the back of my tongue, sour with bile and memory. The light caught the blade's edge, making it glow a lurid, sickly yellow. For a second, every shred of bravado cracked right down the center, pure animal panic shrieking inside my skull.

This was it. The end.

Sweat stung my eyes. As he moved to press the blade to my throat, I looked him dead in the eye for a final, desperate gamble. I could feel the heat of the metal, the press of his claws locking my chin in place. My heart hammered, a drumbeat of pure defiance.

"Kill me, then," I sneered, my voice louder than a scream. "But he'll find you. And when he's done, there won't be enough of you left to feed the lava serpents."

I saw the moment doubt undercut his arrogance, saw the flicker of uncertainty. I held his gaze, refusing to flinch.

For half a heartbeat, silence reigned. I watched the possibility of my own death reflected in his eyes, my fear boiling hot and proud in my chest.

A roar didn't just shatter the air. It tore the world apart. A sound of incandescent rage, a promise of utter annihilation that vibrated through the rock and into my bones.

Draskeer stumbled back.

My whole body jerked and I lunged as far away from him as I could. The ground trembled. The roar ripped through the volcanic hush, primal violence made unstoppable. Heat and wind slammed my back, gritty sand biting my skin.

Omvar landed between us.

He didn't crash. He impacted. A cataclysm of red scales and furious power, his wings flaring wide like molten banners, kicked up a storm of dust and stones that stung my face.

He was wounded, a dark gash weeping blood down his side, but he seemed not to notice. The scent of him slammed into me—smoke and honey and blood, the impossible comfort of safety and danger fused as one. His entire being was a weapon aimed at the Drakarn who held me.

Draskeer stumbled back, his arrogant smirk wiped away by a flash of disbelief, then raw, feral hatred. He shoved me away. I fell hard.

Pain flared along my wrists, elbows, and shoulders. The hot sand bit into my side, and for an instant, the world whirled, broken. I gasped, struggling not to choke on the grit clogging my throat.

But even through the haze of pain, some wild, battered spark flared inside me.

Omvar didn't look at me. He didn't dare. His focus was absolute, his body a coiled spring of lethal intent. A low, continuous growl rumbled in his chest, a sound that promised a slow, painful death.

I forced myself up, scraping my knees raw, just to see. I felt small. Exposed. Trapped.

Predator versus predator.

And I was the prey caught between them.

23

OMVAR

THIS BASTARD THOUGHT he could take my mate?

He was already dead. He just didn't know it yet.

Every thought, every wound, every memory was gone. Burned away in the killing heat that roared in my blood. The world narrowed to the space between me and Draskeer. The roar that tore from my throat wasn't a sound; it was the mate-bond given voice, a promise of annihilation that shook the stone beneath my claws.

Heat hammered the volcanic plain, the ground shivering with tension beneath the red sky. Sulfur stung my nose, the air shimmering with the poison of old eruptions and the scarlet haze of twin suns. Grit scoured my scales as the wind screamed across obsidian spires, slicing every exposed inch of flesh.

I crashed down in a storm of dust, and rock exploded outward as my wings flared. A cataclysm of fury bellowed inside me. The gash in my side wept blood, a hot, sticky track down my scales, but the pain was a distant thing, not even an inconvenience. Nothing penetrated the tunnel-vision that fixed Draskeer in my sights.

My entire being was a weapon, honed and aimed at the male who dared to touch what was mine.

He shoved her aside. Reika stumbled and fell, a small, fragile thing against the unforgiving rock.

My body jerked to go to her, but I didn't dare. I couldn't look at her for more than a second. To see her fear, her pain, would shatter my focus and risk it all. My gaze locked on Draskeer, a predator's stare, absolute and lethal. A low, continuous growl rumbled in my chest. The ground vibrated with it.

I would give him a slow, very painful death.

His feet slid back, heels grinding black grit as he saw me. The arrogant smirk disappeared from his face, replaced by a flash of disbelief, then a vicious hatred that mirrored my own. Sweat gleamed at the edge of his jaw, and his tail bristled, scraping the scorched stone.

We circled. Two monsters locked in a deadly

dance. The prize: a small, unbroken human, braver than any warrior I'd ever known. The heat pressed in, suffocating; the sulfur thick enough to taste on my tongue. Wind clawed at my wings, swirling dust and embers in angry spirals. I watched his every step, every twitch of claw and tail.

He let the silence stretch, then rolled his shoulders, finding his bravado. The play-actor from the arena, remembering his audience. Skorai's dog could never resist the theater. He flicked the blade in his hand, letting the desert sun catch on the jagged edge. The scent of old blood hung on him like a shroud.

"You were always soft. Even in the pits, you never had the stomach for the real work," he sneered, his blade glinting.

I didn't answer. Words were a weakness I couldn't afford. I let his taunts wash over me, fuel for the fire. The bond screamed in my blood. Protect her. End him.

He wanted me to lose control, to go wild and make mistakes. I wouldn't give him the satisfaction. My claws curled into the ashen ground until the rock cracked, my arms tight, wings hunched with the promise of violence.

We crashed together, blades drawn, metal

clanging so hard the echo split the sky. He pressed, I forced back, the weapons scraping scales and skin. The clangs became a drumbeat in my chest.

Fury. Focus.

Every step thundered, every breath harsh and dry as the desert wind.

He was good. Cunning. He feinted, drawing me in, and his claws caught me high on the shoulder, grating against bone. Pain, white-hot and blinding, lanced through me. I roared in agony and fury and hit back with a sweep of my tail. He staggered back.

But he recovered too quickly.

He came in low, under my guard, and a searing pain exploded in my already wounded side. My leg buckled. I went down to one knee, the world tilting, the red sky spinning. My vision flickered to gray at the edges.

Draskeer stood over me, his chest heaving, a triumphant, bloody grin splitting his face. "The great champion of Ignarath," he spat. "Brought to his knees."

My claws dug trenches in the stone, the ground biting back with heat and grit. My head pounded, my throat burning with each ragged breath.

This was it. He was going to end me.

The wind screamed, cutting through pain and panic. Blood dripped down my side, hot, sticky, burning where it tracked through the torn flesh beneath my scales. I could taste it, my own blood in my mouth, an iron sting that threatened to drown my senses. The shame was hot and choking. I'd come to save her, and instead I was broken, spent, prey on my knees just like in the old days, just like the monster I swore never to be.

But then there was a flicker of movement from behind him. Reika. She was on her feet, her face a mask of terror and reckless courage. She snatched a jagged piece of obsidian from the ground.

"Hey, asshole!" she screamed.

Draskeer turned, distracted for a fraction of a second.

It was all I needed.

Rage surged through my bones. The beast inside me tore at its leash, demanding blood. For her. For every moment of fear, every wound, every chain. I let the fury burn away the pain. Muscles bunched, legs trembling. I forced myself upright in a single, violent motion.

I didn't think. Didn't aim for a clean kill. I aimed to maim, to break, to make him suffer for every second of fear he put in her eyes.

My claws slashed out, catching his arm at the elbow, bone crunching, scales splitting, flesh tearing under the force of my blow. Draskeer screamed, the sound sharp and desperate. I followed, relentless, my tail whipping low and hard, connecting with the joint of his leg, shattering it with a sickening crack. His body collapsed, writhing, pain blooming across every inch of his monstrous face.

He lashed out blindly, claws raking my chest, his fangs snapping for my throat. I grabbed his head, slamming it into the rock.

I wanted him to beg.

I wanted him to bleed the way Reika had bled on Ignarath's stones.

The world was a blur of red and heat and violence.

He was on the ground, whimpering, the bravado gone, replaced by the animal fear of the dying. I stood over him, my chest heaving, blood dripping from a dozen wounds. The beast in me wanted to tear his throat out with my teeth.

But Reika was watching.

I forced the animal in me back, forced the urge down until I was trembling with the effort. My claws hovered over his throat, the promise of anni-hilation, but I didn't strike. Not yet. I looked up and saw her standing, hair wild, obsidian shard still clutched in her hand, terror and defiance shining in her eyes.

She was alive. And she was my judge.

I delivered the final, clean blow, ending it. The silence that followed was deafening, broken only by the wind whistling over the rocks and our own ragged breathing.

For a heartbeat, the world hung still. The bond roared in my blood, demanding assurance, demanding proof that she was untouched, unbroken.

Then the adrenaline crashed, and the pain hit me all at once. My legs trembled. I swayed, the world going gray at the edges. The agony in my side flared, a molten spear of suffering. The wounds along my shoulder and chest throbbed, blood trickling over my scales in rivulets, the smell of it sharp as rust. Breathing was an effort.

I turned to Reika. She was staring at me, her eyes wide, her body shaking. She took a step toward me, and her legs gave out.

I caught her before she hit the ground, my arms closing around her small, trembling body. She collapsed against me.

Her heart hammered against my chest, wild and

frantic. Her skin felt clammy, her breath shaky with the aftermath of terror and relief. I bent my head, pressing my jaw against her hair, grounding myself in the reality of her, alive and safe in my arms.

We clung to each other, battered, bloodied, unsteady. I could taste the salt of her sweat, the tang of my own blood on the wind. I forced my wings to wrap us both, shielding her from the furnace wind that scoured the plain, from the hostile emptiness that threatened to swallow us whole. She buried her face in my chest, fingers clinging to the ragged edge of my torn scales.

Above the rush of blood in my own ears, I heard the beat of wings, low, steady, a promise in the air. I lifted my head and saw Khorlar and other Scalvaris warriors descending, their forms carving shadows against the red sky.

Safety. Closure. The world would keep turning, for now.

But for that one endless moment, the only thing that mattered was the fact that my mate was alive, clinging to me, not flinching from my touch but pressing close, her strength, her courage, her wild, unbroken spirit all woven together with my own battered hope.

My mate was safe. That was all that mattered.

THE WORLD SWAM back into focus through a haze of pain and the cloying, metallic scent of healing herbs. I was lying on a stone slab, but it was warm, radiating a deep, steady heat that seeped into my bones. The air was thick with steam and the low murmur of voices.

The healing caverns.

Panic cut through me, sharp and immediate, banishing the dizzy unreality for one vicious heartbeat. The pain in my body didn't matter. The confusion, the strangeness of waking in a place I'd never meant to return to, all of it shrank to a single, clawing need.

Where was he?

I tore through my own fog, muscles screaming

in protest as I tried to push myself upright. My heart crashed against my ribs with wild, panicked urgency, a single name hammering itself into shape from the fragments of my waking thought. Not me. Not my wounds. Not even my own survival. Just one thing mattered.

"Omvar?" My voice cracked, ragged and raw at the edges from too many unreleased screams.

A hand pressed gently but firmly on my shoulder, impossibly strong and impossibly tender at once. My skin stung under the contact, hot-cold and electric, my nerves skittering with the ancient memory of claws in the dark.

"He is here, little one. And so are his wounds. Lie still."

I blinked, vision clearing in fits and starts. Light trembled and stuttered along the cavern walls, painted amber and bloodred by clusters of heat crystals embedded in the stone. Steam curled like living ghosts, softening the world's edges, half-hiding bodies at rest and others in too much distress.

Mysha, the elder Drakarn healer, loomed above me. Her scaled face was all gruff concentration, years etched in every line, not a trace of softness unless you looked for it in the careful way her brows drew together. Her claws, lethal and precise as scalpels, dabbed a pungent, mossy poultice onto a cut on my arm. The sting of it made me flinch, not enough to draw a sound, but she felt it anyway. Her gaze was relentless, searching my face for weakness I didn't want to betray.

The cavern stretched out, vast and echoing, every inch breathing the sharp tang of medicinal herbs layered over the constant, mineral bite of scorched stone and sulfur. The floor was lost under curls of steam, with stone slabs like islets scattered in the haze, each one occupied. The low chorus of groans and soft Drakarn voices drifted beneath the ceaseless hiss of steam vents.

Across the cavern, half-shrouded by the gold and red flicker, Omvar was being tended to by two other healers. Seeing him stripped to the waist sent a jolt through my chest.

His massive wings were a roadmap of fresh, weeping gashes and older, silvered scars. He sat rigid, jaw clamped tight, as they worked, every muscle a line of stubborn resistance, not a sound escaping him. My heart lurched in my chest, torn between the shape of him and the memory of everything I'd almost lost.

"He's … is he going to be okay?"

Mysha snorted, a dry, rattling sound that vibrated somewhere deep in her chest. "He'll live. The same reckless idiocy I see in every mated pair. You get the scent in your head and forget how to duck." She jabbed a claw in my direction, the tip glistening with poultice and something darker beneath. "And you. You are lucky. Mostly bruises and scrapes. Your champion, however, was less fortunate."

I winced, both at her words and the bite of the bitter moss. The sting wasn't just physical this time. Guilt crawled up my throat, a shameful, burning ache that threatened to choke me. Every old fear screamed: This is on you. He bled, because of you.

"It's my fault." The confession slipped out, brittle and small, hardly more than a whisper.

"It's always your fault," another voice said, laced with dry humor that almost made me flinch. Nyx lounged against a nearby pillar, arms crossed, his stormy scales seeming to drink the light. He looked entirely too relaxed for someone who'd just been in a battle. "If it wasn't for you humans, we'd all be sitting around, bored, waiting for the lava to boil over. So, thank you for the entertainment."

Despite the situation, a weak smile touched my lips. There was something almost comforting in the ritual of Nyx's sarcasm, a reminder that even in a place like this, there was room for the familiar sting of banter. Sarcasm could be a lifeline.

The next hour was a blur of gentle, efficient care. Mysha's claws moved with surprising delicacy, peeling off filthy bandages and layering new ones with expert speed. Her running commentary never stopped, a constant drizzle of scold and wry observation that somehow felt like a form of protection all its own.

Each time she pressed a fresh poultice to my bruised ribs, she muttered dire warnings about humans and their fragile parts, as if I'd gone out and gotten myself nearly killed just to ruin her evening.

All the while, Nyx kept up a steady stream of asides, his tail flicking lazily against the pillar, eyes gleaming with the predatory humor the Drakarn seemed to specialize in. His words bit, but they never wounded. I got the sense that as far as he was concerned, if you could survive his jokes, you could survive anything.

"Honestly," Mysha muttered, wrapping a fresh bandage around my wrist with a precision that belied her gruffness, "the trouble this mating bond causes. More work for me than a decade of war.

Rath and his scientist, now this one." She gestured vaguely at Omvar with her chin. "At least the Warrior Lord had the sense to get his wounds treated before rutting."

My face flushed hot. I could feel it rise, crawling from my chest to my ears, a wave of mortification that nothing in this world could disguise. Mysha didn't seem to care, and snorted, the sound bouncing off the stone as if it carried a secret joke only the old and the stubborn got to share.

Nyx coughed to cover a laugh, the effect ruined by the way his eyes sparkled with mischief. I shot him a glare, but it landed weakly. Worn smooth by pain and embarrassment, I could hardly summon the energy for my usual barbs.

My own injuries were, per Mysha's assessment, nothing but bruises and scrapes. An insult, really, next to Omvar's wounds. Once I was cleaned and dressed, my left arm swaddled in sticky bandages and my ribs cinched tight with some fire-scented wrap, I swung my legs slowly off the slab. My muscles screamed in protest, a symphony of ache and stubbornness, but I ignored them.

I wasn't going to ask permission. I didn't need approval to see him.

I pushed myself upright, determined, and

hobbled across the cavern, each step slow and uncertain, but mine. The stone beneath my feet radiated heat, as if the world itself was trying to urge me forward.

Omvar sat at the edge of another slab, still and monumental, his massive wings slung like torn banners behind him. The healers packed up their tools, giving me a wide berth, their knowing glances sliding between us and then away. What were they thinking? That I was a fool, or that I was brave? Did it matter?

He looked up as I approached. Those gold eyes tracked my every step. He didn't move. Didn't speak. Just watched, his face an impassive mask, unreadable. I stopped in front of him, my hands twisting in the hem of my tunic. My tongue stuck to the roof of my mouth, every word I'd tried to conjure suddenly shriveled and useless.

Thank you felt too small. I'm sorry felt like a lie.

I love you?

I wasn't sure how to get those words out at all.

So I did the only thing I could think of. I reached out and gently touched the edge of a newly stitched wound on his shoulder, my fingers tracing the line of it. He flinched, a brief tremor under my touch, but he didn't pull away.

"You came for me."

"Always," he rumbled, his voice low and rough.

The ache inside me loosened, the last of the fear, the last of the shame, finally beginning to recede. I wasn't hiding behind him. I was standing with him.

I stayed by his side as he recovered, a silent, stubborn presence. I helped him drink water, the coolness of the ceramic mug sweating against my hand as I lifted it to his lips. I adjusted the blankets around his shoulders, tucking one edge over the jagged line of a fresh wound. Each act was small, ordinary, but together they felt monumental, a rebuilding in miniature, the slow, careful architecture of trust.

We didn't talk much, not about what mattered, anyway. We just breathed together, letting the silence spread and settle, not absence, but comfort. Even in the silence, I felt the bond humming, an unbreakable thread that tied us, more powerful than language, more dangerous than pain. There was something deeply right about not needing to fill the air with words.

The world faded, the pain faded, everything but him faded. I let myself lean into his heat, my shoulder pressed to his arm, feeling the steady thrum of his pulse under scales marked by more scars than I could count. Each one a story. Each one a survival.

Nyx eventually made his way over, his stride lazy, his eyes glinting with mischief and a rare, dangerous kind of respect.

"As touching as this is, the Council will want a report. Try not to get into any more trouble before I get back." He gave Omvar a look that was almost respect. "Good kill."

He didn't look at me, not directly, but the ghost of a smirk slid over his lips before he turned away. Some perverse instinct made me want to stick my tongue out at his retreating back, the small, childish urge almost strong enough to cut through the haze of pain.

As Nyx left, Mysha returned, carrying two steaming mugs in her scaly, unhurried hands. The scent reached me first: sharp, pungent, bitter as defeat, with an undercurrent of something sweet and dangerous. I took the offered mug with both hands, the warmth soaking into my bruises like the promise of waking up whole.

She handed one to Omvar without ceremony. "Drink. It will help with the pain." She looked from me to Omvar, a faint, grudging approval in her old eyes.

"I want you both to rest. And take it easy." She paused, and the corner of her mouth twitched. "Not that patience is a virtue found in most mated pairs."

I couldn't help it, a laugh escaped, raw and battered, too small to be real, but alive all the same. Omvar's mouth curled at one edge, the motion barely there but unmistakable. We sat side by side, battered, silent, our hands cradling hot mugs. The world shrank to the slow, steady thrum of our breathing, the aching, impossible comfort of belonging.

For the first time in a long time, I let myself believe in it.

PEACE.

The word was foreign on my tongue, a concept I'd only ever understood by its absence. For two days, there was peace. My wounds still ached, a dull, persistent fire beneath my scales, but it was a clean pain. An honorable pain. It was the price of her safety, a cost I would pay a thousand times over.

But now we were finally back in our quarters.

The thought sent a jolt of possessive satisfaction through me, so potent it felt almost like a physical blow. The air was warm, thick with the scent of healing herbs and the sweetness of her skin.

She was there. She was whole.

I let that truth fill me, staring at the low, golden flicker of heat crystals embedded in volcanic rock.

Shadows clung to the corners and pooled under the battered table where a mug still waited, half-filled with bitter, cooling herbal slurry.

The quiet between us was charged, heavy with unspoken things, the violent memory of the battle and the shared aftermath of the healing caverns. Every time my gaze met hers, a current arced between us. It had been too long since I'd tasted her.

I watched her as she moved about the room, her small human frame dwarfed by massive stone furniture. She was restless, her hands fiddling with the hem of her tunic, her eyes darting to the door and back to me. The memory of the attack was still a ghost in the room, a shadow at the edge of her vision.

I wanted to erase it. To burn it away with a different kind of fire.

So I waited. I sat on the edge of the sleeping platform, claws curled inward to keep myself from reaching for her, biting back the raw need that stretched my patience closer to breaking than any wound ever had. I drank her in—every flick of her fingers, the subtle shift of her hips in my space, the way she looked at the room now, comfortable, not like she was planning her escape route.

A bitter smile twisted the corner of my mouth.

When I'd first brought her there, she'd eyed the door like an injured animal, ready to bolt at the smallest opening. Now she moved with unthinking ownership, leaving traces of herself scattered everywhere: the slight indentation where she'd set her satchel, a smear of honey on the rim of the mug, the fresh herbal scent that had replaced the iron tang of blood.

I almost wanted to thank my enemies for threatening her, for forcing her into my care, for giving me this: her, alive in my space, not running. It was a savage, twisted debt, but I felt it all the same. Gratitude coiled through me, hot and brief as lightning.

She turned. Looked at me. Her eyes were full of heat. Full of want.

She walked toward me and didn't stop until she stood directly between my knees.

"Your scars," she whispered, her voice a little rough. "I want to see them."

The words hit deeper than any blade ever had. She didn't ask to see the clean lines of victory or the old wounds faded with time. She wanted the whole truth, what I was, what I had survived, what I could not, or would not, hide.

She reached out and brushed against the fabric

of my tunic. The touch was nothing, a whisper through worn cloth, but I felt the sensation straight down to my cock. My breath hitched, a punch of need tightening every muscle.

I went still. My breath caught in my throat. I didn't show my scars to anyone. They were a map of my shame, of every failure, every life I'd taken, every piece of myself I'd sold to survive Ignarath.

But Reika was mine.

And she owned every part of me.

Slowly, I shrugged out of my tunic. The air of the room, usually warm, felt cold against my bare scales. I felt exposed, stripped of more than just cloth.

She drank in the sight of me, eyes roaming from my throat to the ridges below my ribs, lingering at the jagged silver scars and sickly pearls where scales had been torn and healed, where talon and blade had sought to kill what refused to die. My shoulders locked, naked and open under her gaze. I held myself completely still. If she wanted the ugly truth, I wouldn't shield it.

Reika's hands lifted, trembling slightly, and her fingers traced the jagged, silvered line of an old blade wound across my chest. Her touch was featherlight, reverent. It didn't feel like judgment. It felt like acceptance.

"You're beautiful," she breathed.

The words shattered something inside me. A wall I hadn't even known was there crumbled to dust.

All the old voices, the ones that whispered monster, beast, killer, fell silent under the touch of her skin, under the weight of her worship. I felt seen—not weighed and found wanting, but counted and claimed.

She pressed her mouth to the scar, a soft kiss that sent fire through my veins. And then her hands were on me, undressing me, her movements no longer hesitant but filled with a fierce, driving need.

The fabric slipped away. My skin prickled in the rush of air, nerves raw and newly bared. She took her time, exploring my body, kissing each scar as if to erase the memory of the pain that had caused it. Every brush of her lips, every graze of her fingers, was a benediction, a slow, deliberate rewriting of every ugly memory.

She moved lower, mouth trailing the seam of flesh along my ribs, hands dancing along the map of pain and survival. A low sound escaped me, half-groan, half-plea. I was stripped—not just of clothes, but of every layer of armor I'd ever grown. All my power, all my violence, gone. Only her worship remained.

She got on her knees. My breath stuttered into silence. I reached out, put my hand on her shoulder to stop her, the urge to shield her still so strong.

"I don't require that, *thravena*."

Her eyes were dark with want. The hunger in them was not desperation, not pity, but promise.

"I do."

There was no room for argument. She undid my pants and stroked my cock before taking me into her mouth.

The sensation was white-hot, a surge of pleasure so sharp it bordered on agony. Her lips were soft, her tongue exploring, the heat of her mouth drawing the blood down, making me throb. Nothing in Ignarath had prepared me for this: not the pit, not the pain, not the mate-bond's relentless, insistent ache. This was worship and surrender, the kind that made every muscle in my body tense with gratitude.

She tasted me, slow at first, then with a boldness that left my thoughts scattered. The slick movement of her tongue, the gentle scrape of teeth, the way her mouth stretched to take me in, inch by aching inch. My hand gripped the edge of the platform, claws digging furrows that would scar the stone.

Her palm slid up my thigh, nails trailing, setting fire along a path of nerves. Her other hand cupped my balls, rolling them with a tenderness that made my tail twitch, desperate to wrap her up, to keep her close. The urge to thrust, to take, roared through me, but I held back, let her set the pace, the rhythm, the depth.

I looked down at her and saw her eyes on me. The question was there, unspoken.

Can I trust you?

Will you break me?

I answered by surrendering completely.

I let her see me shiver. I let her feel the tremor running through me, the way I would do anything for her pleasure, for her forgiveness. My mate was a gift. Her courage, her want, her hands on me, around me—these were everything I'd ever craved, and everything I never believed I deserved.

She sucked me deep, throat fluttering around the head of my cock, her lips sliding down the length, letting the mobile lip at the tip rub against her tongue. I groaned, a ragged, broken sound, not caring how desperate it made me. My hips jerked, restrained only by the last shreds of my control.

She didn't flinch. She took me to the root, the heat of her mouth tightening, her jaw aching, but refusing to let go. Her hair brushed my thighs, her hands holding me as if I would vanish if she eased her grip for a moment.

I moaned, the sound guttural and raw. If there had been pain, I would have welcomed it. Instead, there was only need—her need, my own, tangled and indistinguishable.

I did everything I could to hold back, to let her have this, to let her take me to the edge again and again. My hands fisted in the bedding, my tail wrapped around her waist, anchoring me to the moment.

I couldn't stop the noise in the back of my throat. "Off, *thravena*, if you don't want this to end now."

She pulled back. Her lips were swollen. Her pupils blown. She looked like she'd been fucked and I now I needed to make good on the promise of that look.

"I need you, *thravena*."

The words snapped whatever self-control I had left. I hauled her up, desperate, and crushed my mouth to hers. Honey and salt and myself on her tongue; I tasted her hunger, her pride, the small, trembling certainty that lived in her hands when she slid them up my chest.

Her legs straddled my lap, knees wide on either side of my thighs. She didn't hesitate. She guided herself over my cock and slowly slid down.

She was in control now, but I shared it with her. I let her set the pace, every motion slow and deliberate, her body taking the thick, ridged length inch by inch.

I was overcome with need for her, every muscle trembling with restraint. I moved slowly, careful not to overwhelm her.

She looked at me, cheeks flushed, hair sticking to her damp forehead. "I'm not going to break."

"But you are precious."

The words tumbled out, a confession, a vow. Her eyes went wide, the last of the fear burning away, replaced by joy, fury, hunger. She braced herself, palms on my chest, and began to move.

We picked up the pace, every stroke a prayer and a challenge. Her hips rolled, finding the rhythm that made her breath catch, her head fall back. I met her, slow at first, then rougher, letting her ride, letting her take, letting her claim me.

It was hot. It was intimate. It was real. I watched the way her chest heaved, the confession on her lips each time she gasped my name, the way her body opened for me, took me deeper, clung to me. My claws raked the bedding, my wings flared, the world narrowed to the place where we joined.

We were fucking, bodies moving in perfect sync. The friction, the stretch, the pressure—it was too much, not enough. I kissed her, open-mouthed, tasting her moans, swallowing her need. My hands slid down her back, cupped her ass, guided her up and down, up and down.

This was intense, the slap of flesh, the slick slide, the heat gathering low and fierce, threatening to consume us both. Each roll of her hips brought me closer, made my vision swim with black and gold and the memory of every pain that had come before.

She rode me faster, chasing the edge, her cunt gripping me in strangling pulses. Her nails dug into my skin, pain and pleasure indistinguishable. My tail wrapped her waist, holding her close. The words spilled out without thought:

"You're mine. Only mine."

She met my thrusts, gasping, "Yours. Always."

We clung to each other, desperate, hungry, shuddering on the edge.

And we finally came together.

It was violent, shattering, her body tightening, milking me, her voice breaking into a sob as she convulsed around my cock. I growled, a raw sound, releasing inside her, every muscle locked, the mate-bond roaring through my veins like fire and mercy.

This was what it felt like to be whole.

To be home.

I held her tighter, my wings instinctively curling around her, a shield against the world outside. She slumped against my chest, breath stuttering, arms winding around my neck. My heart hammered, wild and grateful, as I pressed my mouth to the damp edge of her hair.

Peace in Scalvaris was a fragile thing. But in that room, we had it, and I wasn't letting go.

THE EARLY PATROL was a special kind of hell. The air in the outer tunnels was hot enough to make a soldier's scales burn, and the silence was so absolute it felt like a weight crushing my skull. I moved through it like a ghost, my claws making no sound on the stone.

The city held its breath. Somewhere in the black, the walls sweated, trickles of mineral water slipping down the carved faces, collecting in shallow pools only the desperate would drink from. We'd bled in these tunnels not two weeks ago, Ignarath's mark still fresh on every mind, a wound that wouldn't clot but would be repaid. The silence was an animal: crouched, teeth bared, waiting for the next snap.

Those Ignarath bastards had left everyone on edge. Darrokar wanted extra patrols, which meant less sleep for me.

Each step along the outer ring caught in the old nerves, a stinging reminder of why I wore the blades at my hip even off shift. My scales itched where the heat crystals dimmed, flickering so weakly their glow could barely scrape the dust from the stones. Above, the ceiling curved low and close. The weight of a city full of bodies pressed down, thicker than the heat.

My duty was to keep this city from bleeding out. That job never ended.

But at least my shift did.

I let the tension slough away—or tried to. The job was a second skin. You kept the sharpness on, or you died. But the edge was blunted today, exhaustion grinding its way into my joints, a kind of restlessness that made me want to crawl out of my own scales.

Nothing helped. Not the patrol. Not the knowledge that we'd lived through worse. Not the promise of sleep when I made it home.

Not when the city was this quiet.

I was making my way back, cutting through a lesser-used market that smelled of stale spices and ozone. Most stalls were shuttered, their owners asleep in their quarters. But a faint light flickered from a stall near the back, one that dealt in repurposed tools and rare minerals.

I let the familiar rhythms guide me: the scrape of my boots on rough stone, the sweep of my tail to balance the heavy air, the routine scan for threats. A flicker of firelight caught in my peripheral vision, drawing my focus despite myself. The tiny market was a nothing place, half the tables abandoned, the others layered in dust, the air thick with the ghost of burned cinnamon and the sour tang of metal.

The silence lived there too. Too thick, too absolute. Not even a rat's claw, or not even a trader's mutter.

That's when I saw her.

A human woman, leaning over the counter, bartering with a surly, green-scaled merchant. She was small, wiry, and had scars that traced a faint, pale map along her jawline.

She shouldn't have belonged there, not in that slice of Scalvaris where danger came in shadows and silence and the wrong kind of glance. But she did. She owned her space like she'd carved it out of the rock with nothing but nerve and pain. Her hair was cropped close, bristling around her skull, shining in the sickly light. Her hand braced on the counter, knuckles white, wrist trembling just enough to show the edge of brittle strength.

Her eyes were watchful, constantly scanning the shadows, her posture coiled with a tension that spoke of old dangers and a deep-seated lack of trust.

I knew that tension. I'd worn it myself, sleepless nights with nothing between me and an enemy's blade but luck and a fistful of promises.

This woman's wariness was different, carved in deeper, older wounds. Her gaze didn't just flicker. It mapped every shadow, anticipating betrayal. She stood crooked, weight favoring one leg.

My instincts, dulled by routine, snapped sharp. A sudden coiling in my gut, a need to get closer, to see her. To smell her.

I didn't know her name, but she had to be one of the human women who lived in the city, even if I didn't recognize her.

Something ancient in me stretched awake. Not lust, not quite. Nothing so polite or manageable.

A predator, deep in the marrow. A coil of hunger and curiosity that bypassed reason, straight to the brainstem. My hands itched. I wanted to step out of the shadow and circle her, nose to skin, to drink in whatever scent clung to her battered, stubborn bones.

Who was she?

I stopped, melting into the shadows of a pillar. It wasn't my business. But there was something about her, a fierce, bold energy that drew my eye.

I hadn't come this way for drama. I was restless, sure, but not stupid. Not reckless.

The merchant sneered, gesturing dismissively at the small, glowing heat crystal on the counter. "The price is the price, human. Take it or leave it."

Her chin lifted. "You'll take ten talins, not fifteen," she said, her voice low and surprisingly steady. "This thing is cracked."

My lips twitched. She had nerve.

It wasn't bravado. She named the game, called the bluff, all with a cadence that had seen violence and decided it wasn't all that special. Her hand flicked across the counter, counting coins, palms stained with an old burn, scars hidden and revealed by the movement. The heat crystal on the slab between them pulsed faintly, dim but stubborn.

I drifted, pressing my body flat against the nearest stone column. My weight barely disturbed the dust, each step measured, predatory, deliberate. I didn't want her to see me. Didn't know why.

As she counted out the coins, her gaze swept the market one last time. It snagged on my shadow, and for a half-second, our eyes locked across the empty square.

Time didn't slow. It stopped.

And her scent hit me.

I inhaled deep and was overwhelmed by her. It was a physical blow. Something potent, undeniable.

How had I not noticed it before?

It bypassed thought, and reason, and went straight to the oldest, most ancient part of my brain.

Mine.

The word was a shock, a brand seared into my soul. My fangs ached. My heart gave a single, brutal kick against my ribs. I had heard the others speak of it—Darrokar, Rath, even the stoic Khorlar. The mate-bond. I'd always thought it was an exaggeration, a poetic term for lust and possessiveness.

I was a fool.

She was staring, mouth parted, a flicker of confusion, of awareness, passing over her face. Her scent, impossible, sweet with something sharp beneath, steel and sunrise and the ash of a world that wouldn't die. It crawled over my skin, invaded the cracks in my discipline. Every old lesson, the

Council's drills, watching others fall into this madness, I'd believed myself immune.

Fate could burn.

Now it was inside me. A wound that could never close.

She looked unsettled, her hand tightening on the crystal. She snatched it from the counter, spun without another word to the merchant, and disappeared into a side tunnel.

For a moment, her absence was a physical pain. The world snapped back into motion, the silence louder than a scream.

I stood frozen, my carefully constructed world tilted on its axis. My patrol, the city's security, the lingering threat of Ignarath, it all faded to a dull, distant hum. There was only the ghost of her scent on the air and the violent, undeniable certainty that had just rewritten my future.

I was a member of the Blade Council. A commander. My life was duty and discipline. I had no time for this. No room for this kind of chaos.

But the bond didn't care about my plans. It was a hook sunk deep in my gut, pulling me in a direction I had never intended to go.

I let out a slow, shaky breath. I could still smell her. Sweetness and steel.

That scent burrowed under my skin, a secret only I could taste. My hands trembled, anger and awe warping together.

Who was she? No one.

Everything.

A human, lost and nearly invisible, and now I would burn a city to find her, to know the sound of her breath, the taste of her skin, the name she used when she was alone and afraid.

I didn't pursue. Not yet. A hunt like this required strategy, not brute force. She was already spooked, a wounded thing ready to bolt at the first sign of a predator.

But the hunt had begun. Whether she knew it or not.

NEED A LITTLE MORE OF OMVAR & REIKA?

Sign up at the link below to **receive a free bonus epilogue!**

Get your free bonus epilogue!

https://katerudolph.net/index.php/omvar-bonus/

———

Thank you so much for reading *Beast of Blood and Ash*!

Your support means the world to me. If you enjoyed the story, it would mean even more if you could take a moment to share your thoughts in a review or leave a rating.

Hearing from readers like you makes all the difference!

———

Nyx's story is coming soon!

———

WHAT TO READ NEXT: CRUX

Prince Crux is in a bind.

When the Dragon King commands Crux find a mate, his days of carefree bachelorhood are over. One trip to a psychic matchmaker and he's on the path to his destiny. But it all comes screeching to a halt when he meets a human woman who lights his inner fire and makes him yearn.

She's got a pair of roller skates and an attitude.

Courtney is supposed to be putting the shambles

of her life back together. Getting abducted by aliens isn't part of the plan. Neither is getting rescued by a scorchingly hot dragon that makes her think of an impossible future. But they have no chance together if they can't first escape a planet full of monsters intent on their destruction.

Read for free today!

Dragon Brides
Dragon Princes. Fierce Women. Love.
Fated mates, fierce women, and dragon princes are
ready to find their mates.
Also available in audio!
Crux
Ranger
Saber
Cipher
Storm
Drake
Asher
Knox
Flint
Pine

———

Guarded by the Shifter

Werewolf. Bodyguard. Mate.
The origins of these shifters are shrouded in
mystery, but they're determined to protect their
mates from any harm that comes their way.
Also available in audio!
Hunting Season

On the Prowl
Stalking Magic
Hungry for the Wolf
Wolf Cursed (novella)
Wolf's Temptation

———

Stealing the Alpha

The thief takes what she wants, but the alpha keeps what's his...

Join shifter thief Mel as she clashes with lion alpha Luke in an explosive trilogy of two opposites who can't keep away from one another.

Also available in audio!

The Alpha Heist
Entangled with the Thief
In the Alpha's Bed

———

Alien Mates: Planet Exile

Guerran is no place for pretty human women. But these alien heroes will protect their mates!

Also available in audio!

Exile's Hunter
Exile's Adored

Zulir Warrior Mates

Kidnapped humans. Alien Warriors. Electric wings.

The Zulir Warrior Mates series brings you human heroines and heroes abducted from Earth who find love – and wings! – with the alien warriors who rescue them.

Also available in audio!

Synnr's Saint
Synnr's Hope
Synnr's Spark
Synnr's Kiss
Synnr's Ride

Mated to the Alien

Fated Mate Alien Romance

Detyens are doomed to die young if they don't find their fated mates.

Follow along as these mated pairs fight off aliens, corrupt dictators, prejudiced humans, pirates, and more! The books can be read or listened to in any order, though some characters show up in multiple stories.

Select books available in audio.

Pick a book and jump into the action today!

Ruwen

Tyral

Stoan

Cyborg

Krayter

Kayleb

Shayn

Braxtyn

Doryan

Dekon

Detyen Warriors

Detya was destroyed a hundred years ago.

These doomed warriors are out to find justice… and their mates.

The Detyen Warriors series brings you kick butt heroines, alpha alien heroes, fated mates, and relationships strong enough to span the galaxy!

The entire series is also available in audio!

Soulless

Ruthless

Heartless

Faultless

Endless

———

Detyen Warrior Outcasts
Fated Mate Alien Romance

These doomed warriors were abandoned by their people and live on the edge. Their mates hold the key to their salvation.

Pick a book and jump into the action today!

Also available in audio!

Dangerous Bond

Intrepid Bond

Wayward Bond

———

Alien Holiday Romance

Christmas… in space????
These alien holiday romances look beyond Earth's winter holidays and ring in the season across the galaxy!
Select titles available in audio.
Snowed in with the Alien Beast
The Alien's Winter Gift
The Alien Reindeer's Wild Ride
Trapped with her Alien Mate

Alien Outlaws

Outlaws, schemes, and love… it's all there in the Alien Outlaws series…
Andie Munster is sick of life on Ixilta, the planet she got dumped on after being abducted from Earth six years ago. And when the mysterious and dangerous Xandr shows up looking for a way off the planet, she's half-prisoner, half-co-conspirator in a wild rush to escape.
Also available in audio!
Rogue Alien's Escape

Rogue Alien's Woman
Rogue Alien's Secret
Rogue Alien's Legacy

———

Find more by Kate Rudolph at www.
katerudolph.net

ABOUT KATE RUDOLPH

KATE RUDOLPH IS a paranormal and sci-fi romance writer who lives in Indiana. She loves writing about kick butt heroines and the steamy heroes who love them. She's been devouring romance novels since she was too young to be reading them and had to hide her books so no one would take them away. She couldn't imagine a better job in this world than writing romances and sharing them with her fellow readers.

If you enjoyed this story, please consider leaving a review.

www.ingramcontent.com/pod-product-compliance
Lightning Source LLC
Chambersburg PA
CBHW061654190726
48289CB00006B/1867